MARCH FORTH FOR NAUGHT

S. MUBASHIR NOOR

AURAQ
PUBLICATIONS

Printed: May, 2021   Cover design: S. Mubashir Noor
Edition: 1st   Typesetting: S. Mubashir Noor
ISBN: 978-969-749-114-8
Price: Rs 1500 PKR, $15 US

www.auraqpublications.com | raabta@auraqpublications.com
@AuraqPublications | @AuraqBooks +92-300-0571-530
Printed and Bound by *Passive Printers* - www.passiveprinters.com

*Dedicated to Jerrica
Mamoona, Momina
Muzammil and
Mudassir*

PART I

 NAYA CHOORAN
OR BUST! 

— Prologue —

Rebel, Rebel

A lonely creature sat under a withered olive tree, watching the world burn below him. He seated cross-legged under its skeletal bole that rooted to the rocky summit of the solitary rust-red butte. Around his sable shoulders draped a shawl formed of the sirocco's fiery sands, and his smooth features strained from a familiar disquiet.

Yonder, from once-lush plains rose pillars of stygian smoke, slithering as angry serpents in the sultry sun-dipped breeze that carried the stench of charred flesh and the plaintive wails of the wretched souls yet breathing. Now and again, the wind too brought with it the bestial roars of the demons wreaking death on another human citadel, their lust for destruction ceaseless.

After centuries of witnessing their savagery, such a sight ought not cause him sorrow, and even so it burdened his soul. It stirred an itch he couldn't scratch, a yearning he didn't comprehend.

Beyond the butte carved as a spear's tip, the world lay in

flames as though it were a villain bespoke for God's wrath. The creature from experience knew that wasn't true. Those scorched to cinders were merely flawed beings let loose in the slippery blind alley called life.

Not so the demons who reveled in their carnage. Of God's creations on heaven and earth, they were the most graceless, the most despicable, and he disgusted at using his sirocco to hide their deeds. Yet as he was, and as Allah willed it, he couldn't question his place in the universe.

An enchanted purple-and-gold rug shot up the precipice and hovered beside him, its frilly hems a thousand tongues licking the air. Atop perched a figure in flowing robes and a plumed headdress of the same motif.

"Simoon, why are you always early?" the warlock Samiri asked, frowning.

The butte's saw-toothed roof shook from the creature's snarl. "What's it to you?"

Samiri didn't retreat, though his droopy string bean mustache twitched and his rug shivered and shrank. "Every time you witness their acts, the sirocco blows like hellfire all year. We're not all mighty djinn, my friend."

Simoon kept his distant look. "I no longer wish to act the funeral shroud to fallen cities. When does this end?"

The warlock cast his vacant gaze to the plains where fire and brimstone reigned. Then he lightly shrugged. "Who knows? We each toil through our divine punishment. Just be glad you're not among men."

Simoon said nothing, but his shawl shone bright as a pocket sun. Samiri's jaw slackened.

"You want to return? Have you gone mad? You realize

their greed wrought their ruin, right?"

The djinn again snarled. "The Walrus, will he know?"

Samiri hunched over and exhaled a deep, slow breath. "You understand what'll happen if you undertake such? Someone like you? I'd rather be a cockroach in hades."

Then he flinched from the djinn's stony stare while the powdery dust round them kicked up and danced as a cyclone in the desert.

Simoon rose to his shapeless feet, towering over the warlock. "My faith is unshakable. I must do this."

Chapter One

The Old Man and the Ragamuffin

My name is not important because I don't have one. At least not a proper one, one I'd proudly share with others. What's essential is you know it was tough acting a 12-year-old man in the boonies. Brutal, if I'm honest. You got every inch of the pain for none of the perks. Not that these were plentiful, even when you hit eighteen. *Naya Chooran*, my hometown, was never one to inspire ambition.

Mother for sure showed no empathy for how I saw myself. Bless her human soul and her careworn vulpine features, she wasted no chance to rag on me: when I couldn't sell my daily quota of cheap hard-shelled candy; when I stole to the town square after sunset to watch the bloody cockfights; or when I tried to befriend my fellow ragamuffins. Matter of fact, she possessed the warmth of a teeth-chattering snow cone.

She picked on me day in, day out because I reminded her of father. I assumed as much since without fail she'd slot him into the rat-tat-tat of cusses spewing out of her pinched, bloodless lips.

Years earlier, he, a professional ne'er-do-well, left our treacherous tin-roofed dwelling to buy sewing threads for her side hustle and never returned. I couldn't fault the man. How many hourly admonitions could anyone take?

In his absence, mother honed her poison tongue into a peerless instrument of torture for which I daily played the strop. Why she saw even a smidgen of him in me, I wasn't sure. Yes, I was free-spirited and whimsical, but how could she compare me to someone who scurried in the opposite direction whenever he sighted me? Besides, I couldn't remember ever conversing with him beyond awkward hellos.

Funnily enough, mother disciplined none of my four siblings; her industrious little angels, she called them. Humph, it wasn't as if they were investment bankers. They too sold sweets; street-to-street, hand-to-hand; but they always brought more money home. I bet the cretins were pick-pocketing the extra cash to keep her favor.

We had a hi-bye relationship, me and my siblings, and they were never around when she reached under her rickety charpoy to pull out dad's flaky leather belt. They looked and acted the same, mini-me versions of her with added cunning, while I was the flat-out rebel. Each had proper names when everyone called me Kalia.

Looking back, my folks should've just stitched a kick-me sign to my *kameez*—my loose collarless shirt. I'd have made more money panhandling as a pitiful wretch than peddling the sugar-coated pebbles I claimed were candy. Good thing my clients were similarly clueless for lack of better fare. Only to the poor can an honest man as I sell counterfeit food.

As for mother, when she wasn't sewing flappy tunics and gauzy dopattas with hands atremble, squinting and swearing at her bent needles, or hustling for new orders from our snooty neighbors, she insisted everything was my fault. She wished I'd never shown up, that I was accursed, that warthogs in the sprawling woods beyond Naya Chooran should've reared me instead.

Each time I held my tongue, aching to retort that swine treated their offspring better than her, that it wasn't my crime the poor birthed more children than they could feed. I didn't appreciate her according me less esteem than the stinky grocer next door with an army of horseflies for pets. Who cared if he donated us his leftover veggies? I had my pride as a man.

But grumbling was unmanly, even if she couldn't understand my predicament. I guess the only thing I learned from father was how not to lose your self-respect. Then again, I wasn't the one who'd spent a decade treading her toxic waters.

It's not that I didn't love mother, I did. She provided the leaky roof and the watery gruel with wafer-thin roti that passed for grub in our house. But I loved her as I did the grizzly cross-eyed homeopath from a few blocks over, who offered only the foulest tasting ground herbs whenever I staggered to his hole-in-the-wall clinic in a feverish daze.

Often, I wondered if in a past life I'd committed crimes so grave this trip round the wheel was karmic payback. Nothing else made sense.

Thing is, no one told me manhood snuck up on you without warning, then bludgeoned you into a pulpy mess. One fine day you're pulling boogers out your nose; uninhibited, unreasonably thrilled, everything around you a joyous quest; and the next you must convince po-faced strangers to buy cheap candy.

No wonder it was easy to find happy pills in Naya Chooran. You just needed to stroll out after dinner and unfailingly you'd run into a pusher at most street corners. They always claimed their creamy oval tablets made you whole again, but I didn't believe them for a second, since to a man they wore the manic look of roof jumpers.

Naya Chooran's a town God could've smote twice over in antiquity, and for good reason. The rich few declared they'd earned Allah's favor and expected the rest of us to show gratitude for our scraps. As far as we knew, their highnesses lived in the clouds, in their palatial hillside bungalows overlooking our noisy labyrinth for rats. Our homes, meanwhile, fixed atop pencil-thin pillars of unpainted bricks to prevent the monsoonal rain from washing away our meager lives.

In our maze, we didn't mark the streets with signs, not us. The murkiness of the open sewers snaking on either side of our skinny lanes offered clues aplenty. Hell, there were times I recognized my block by counting the number of cow pies slapped to house walls, or failing that, the density of vermin corpses floating in the sewage.

And a dusty haze hung over town year-round: so dense it was hard to tell the seasons apart, sometimes even morning from midday. Now and then it puckishly whipped up dust devils as tall as streetlights that spun and spun with poly bags and cigarette stubs.

Mother always blamed me for the weather, claiming it arrived with yours truly. Hah, what a crock! If I were a powerful demon, she'd never dare look upon me so poorly.

Good thing I wasn't one to dwell on misery or I'd have popped the happy pills myself. I knew Allah had bigger plans for me, a sense of destiny born of a recurring dream that kept me going despite my troubles.

Now I confess the dream was weird, stunningly so. For weeks every night, I drifted through a blooming field under golden skies that swirled with a heady fragrance. A garden unlike any I could imagine, a garden in glorious technicolor.

Barefooted, I'd pad over lush blades of grass that tickled my soles, my fingertips kissing the daffodils and petunias rowing the endless seedbeds. It carried on and on, infinite, an ocean of green melting into a blonde welkin.

An unmarked arched door awaited me each time: paneled in teal and bounded by knotty creeper vines. And a man always stood to its side, his arms tied behind his back. My doppelganger.

Though he was wiry and two heads taller, he shared my dark complexion, my nest of unruly corkscrew curls, my cleft chin, and my flat fleshy nose. Yet his eyes were different: sharper and self-assured, his irises bouncing colors as an iridescent oil slick.

Many questions gushed forth from my lips. Why was he my mirror? Why I kept pulling into the same dream? But he'd keep mum, wanly smiling and gesturing toward the door.

My heart raced when I pulled on its thick bronze ring, anticipating a great boon but only finding disappointment. Beyond lay a dull gray wall carved with deep splits and deeper claw marks; as if an ambush of tigers used it nightly for a communal scratching post. And strewn at its base were two brilliant gold coins engraved with runic symbols I couldn't decode.

I'd slyly pocket them and reach out to caress the wall's weathered surface, but right after a capful of wind whooshed out its pores, stinging my cheeks and yanking me into reality. Again, I'd revive on the lumpy mattress that clung to my slender frame, my ratty *salwar kameez* soaked in sweat, my loot sadly missing. Curiously, the dream always ended around dawn, and then it was time to earn my keep.

I'd ransack yesterday's leftovers for breakfast, which most mornings were cardboardy pieces of flatbread dipped in pickled garlic, and then roam the sandy streets of my neighborhood selling candy in a stringy wicker basket.

That day was different, though. It changed everything I understood of life.

A dry summer day, if I recall right, because the haze wrung every ounce of moisture from the air and singed my skin extra crisp. A late Friday afternoon, too, as most shops wore their shutters and slavering street dogs outnumbered the locals strolling through our tunnellike lanes.

I was weaving through Naya Chooran's streets as usual, the wicker basket cradled in the crook of my arm, absently hopping over puddled mud and muck. The dream again preoccupied me, and as a result I'd sold few sweets.

Despite my frequent attempts to convince mother, she didn't agree I should switch to selling potato chips or fried pulses. I kept telling her our neighbors were too bitter to have a sweet tooth, but her own bitterness prevented her from seeing reason.

Before I knew it, a flash of light blinded me. No sooner had I shaded my eyes that a white projectile was scudding toward my throat.

My breath cinching, I jerked away from its path, but in vain. A tennis ball wrapped in electrical tape boxed me flush on the nose and shoved me backward.

My basket flung skyward, and for a nanosecond the candies suspended aloft before scattering as confetti onto the asphalt. And to my horror, a handful slipped into the sewer and sank into its tarry gunk.

Round twenty feet away, the stout kid froze in a cover-drive pose; his sheeny oatmeal-white bat and elbows raised high, a smug grin lighting his fishlike lips. Afi: the town councilor's son and consummate backyard bully. Likewise, the patron saint of hair gel so his scalp shone as a watermelon dunked in grease.

I cussed through my clenched teeth. Was it his shiny dome or the paddlelike willow that stunned me for a shake? Argh, these local thugs and their blasted cricket.

In colorful shorts they descended as a swarm of locusts, crowing at dumb jokes, and slapping each other's backsides. They'd block whatever street on a whim, spray-paint lines on the blacktop to mark their territory, and treat passersby as pinatas.

I'd be lying if I said I didn't wish to partake, but unlike those waifs, I had responsibilities. I was a man.

While Afi and his cronies tittered, my shock swapped for white-knuckled fury. If I were Medusa, I'd have shaped my greasy curls into shoulder-length snakes and cast the unholy lot into stone.

I dropped to my haunches and duckwalked to one by one replace the unsoiled sweets. Then I snapped to my feet and squared my shoulders. "Watch where you're hitting," I said, my finger stabbing at him.

Afi stuck the bat upright between a crack in the road, and he leaned on its handle, sneering. "Act a man, runt."

Then, holding my incredulous stare, he over and over slashed his blade through the air, repeating the stroke that nearly decapitated me. This wasn't the first time he'd tried to rile me up, the uppity gorilla.

A few days earlier, he and his thugs accosted me two lanes over and dumped trash on my head. They took off, cackling, before I could raise my dukes, but not today. Whatever he was compensating for by acting obnoxious was not my problem. If he grew up motherless, I'd gladly gift him mine.

My coiled fists raised to my chest, the blood in my ears boiling. "*Wah*, I work like a mule all day and you dare question my manhood?"

Afi kept smirking while his gang chuckled away. I stepped sideways to stow my basket on the top step of the bodega stuck with a for-sale sign, noting the maple leaf-shaped scar on the lamppost nearby.

Then I yanked up the sooty cuffs of my kameez. "No matter how many limbs I lose today, you're all crawling home without a leg," I barked and stomped headlong at them.

Once more the taped ball shot toward me, and I braked to pouch it in my palms. Smacking the pavement so often had made it coarse to the touch, its lacquered surface slivering.

Afi's butt wriggled as he retook his batting stance before three upstanding steel rebars soldered together as stumps, his angled bat hanging beside his hips. Then with brisk nods he beckoned me to bowl at him.

"Since you're so poor, knock back the wickets in two tries and I'll pay you for the sweets. Mere pocket change for me, he-he."

He signaled to his posse, who forthwith arranged into fielding positions round the pitch and threw me mirthful glances.

I yearned to snatch the rebars and beat Afi's sneer into a saucepan, but he was a head taller and built as a heifer.

And though I earlier spoiled for a fight, winning a brawl won't return my sweets. I'd just live through mother's belting later and tomorrow go farther into town to make up the lost sales.

"Fine," I said, scowling. In that moment, a thunderbolt to his kisser was my reason for living.

After retreating a few paces from the bowling-end stumps, I tossed my locks back and windmilled my arm. Wasn't much of a cricketer, but given a slingshot, I could nail a marble anywhere from ten feet away. That's how I saved up for funnel cakes in a town brimming with compulsive gamblers.

My ticker flam-flammed as a snare drum while the crows perched aloft on the lattice of half-naked power lines fluttered their charcoal wings and cawed louder. They must have sensed blood. The heifer's, hopefully.

The toe of Afi's bat kept tapping the road in a leaky faucet rhythm, his forehead creased in concentration, his cronies yelling encouragements. I drew a long breath, readying to rev up to the bowling crease.

TAK-TAKA-TAK-TAKA-TAK. BURRAHHH!

My focus shattered from the sudden clatter of dhol beats and Punjabi hollers, which caused the crows to squawk angrily and evacuate en masse.

From up the drive, where the track met a cropland of turnips and potatoes, an old man sporting a perky turban neared us doing the *luddi* dance: his upraised arms pumping in the air while he hopped one-legged with the other tucked at the knee. A lava-gray boom box slung over his chest, bobbing in time with his shimmies, and he waved to an invisible crowd on both sides of the street.

While we goggled at him speechlessly, the geezer pranced to the center of our pitch and hit stop on his stereo.

Once the flashing neon lights ringing its speakers died, his head tipped to one side as he cupped an ear. "Eh, where's the welcoming committee?"

Rows of chipped corn-yellow teeth peeked from under his playful grin, while his sunken cheeks hugged a scraggly beard sopped in lurid henna. His eyes hid behind blocky aviators, fashionable at first, until you noted the twists of transparent tape holding the arms fast to the frame.

You just didn't see strangers of his stripe in this town, or I doubted anywhere outside a loony bin.

Afi's bat smacked his sneaker while he stared daggers at the old-timer. "What's your problem? Who are you?"

Personally, I was inches from snatching the blade and whacking the geezer's gut for ruining my sweet revenge. Even for a blind man, he was mightily pushing his luck.

His chin rolled toward Afi, his slight underbite parted in surprise. Then he pushed his shades up his large doughy nose and buttoned his polka-dotted waistcoat, the corners of his mouth upturned in conceit. "Chacha Kakakhel, of course. Your new councilor."

"What?" Afi asked, grimacing, trading murderous looks with his cronies.

The toasty air round us was still until the ball slipped from my clammy grip and bounced on the asphalt. Their eyes set on me at once.

"Ah, are you boys playing cricket?" Chacha asked. "Come now, I'll open the match like all important people do." He outspread his bony palm and waited.

"Vamoose, we're in the middle of a game," Afi spat back, leveling his bat at the geezer.

"Yea! We got no time for you," I said, eager to repay the gorilla for his insolence.

Chacha broke into the most insane laugh, which to my ears resembled a whistling train chasing after a honking seal. "You chicken, kids? And here I thought you were men."

I tugged on my curls as if they were the geezer's leathery neck, and Afi's countenance flushed crimson. Then the gorilla showed an unexpected bout of charity, or maybe his intentions were similarly fatal.

Afi closed his eyes, his bosom heaving from deep breaths. Then he shot me a curt thumbs-up and lined up before the stumps. "Go ahead then," he told Chacha. "Let's see what you got."

I frowned at him but followed instructions. Though I pined for revenge, a curious giddiness possessed me. A blind codger who'd announced he was the new councilor and could play cricket? I'd never hear a better punchline.

I warily strode up to Chacha and palmed him the ball, to which he patted my head, grinning. Then I brusquely nudged him toward the stumps, but to my surprise, the geezer detoured to where I'd placed my basket and set his boom box right beside it.

Then he toddled back and nearly impaled his crotch on the steel rebars. A brief squeal later, he grabbed his family jewels and skipped round in circles while we giggled. But soon he recovered, juggling the ball and coolly glancing our way as if he were Imran Khan in his pomp.

The other kids, simpering, ganged together as wicketkeepers, in wait of him tumbling onto the blacktop and splitting his skull open. But I retreated to behind Chacha's bowling arm, concluding it was the safest place if he lost control. My schnoz still stung from the blow earlier, and surely another one could flatten it into a *pakora*—a spiced fritter.

More so, I owned no appetite for drinking any more of the homeopath's noxious syrups. I'd sooner rent a funeral shroud and dig a grave.

Chacha's fists joined, and he kept shaking the ball while muttering to himself, puffing at it again and again as though it were a steaming plate of biryani.

My brow hiked high at his shenanigans. Was he praying he'd not make a fool of himself? Hah, that ship had long sailed.

Then Chacha's leg lifted and his arm cocked back in a catapult pose. At the same time Afi's fingers flexed over the carmine bat handle and his taut trunk tipped forward, his peepers large as tangerines.

"Allahu Akbar," Chacha cried as his hand whipped past his chest in a chucking motion.

Afi swung wildly, twice for effect, but there was no sound. I blinked on repeat and scrubbed my brows. The ball left the geezer's wrist and then it vanished!

It didn't ping an electric pole; crash into a house window; thump the drain pipes protruding from every roof; or smack into any unfortunate sap loafing in the lane. How?

Before long, Afi and fiends were rolling on the road from belly laughs, their fingers pointing to the sky. Chacha spun round and walked away without comment, his features unruffled as if the gaffe were part of his plan.

I felt for him, how could you not when a deranged man tried to act normal, but the missing ball absorbed my thoughts. Gravity should've made it land by now.

I ambled over to Afi's spot and peered heavenward, squinting to pry past the dusty brume coating the atmosphere.

A white dot. It haloed from the diffuse sunlight, growing bigger and bigger, its descent bringing on a faint whine.

My legs tingled in sync with my galloping pulse. This was no tennis ball.

I made a mad dash away from the pitch, the ticktick of a time bomb starting in my head, the Shahada pouring out my quivering lips.

Seconds later, right where I'd been standing, a cone-shaped missile the size of a wheelbarrow cratered the road.

Chapter Two

Another One's Coming!

I was sprinting away from the pitch, huffing enough oxygen for an interstellar trip, my vision black-spotted and fuzzy.

Over and over I glimpsed behind me, my pop-eyes tracing the missile hurtling toward the road while shapeless figures scurried in different directions. And though my ears rang as a fire drill, the rocket's wail was deafening.

The dusty haze was an ice pick goring my lungs, and yet harder and harder I sucked in breaths to sustain my pumping limbs. Doubtless I'd fare better at this enterprise if only the planet-sized lump in my throat didn't swell with every passing second.

There was an almighty crash, and the earth madly pitched and rolled. I was a pinball rattling inside a soda can.

One instant my feet were pounding the blacktop, and the next an irresistible force seized me. I was its hand puppet, soaring sideways over the asphalt and slamming spine-first into a concrete landing.

My body forthwith set on fire, and tears flooded my cheeks. I was writhing on the road, howling from pain, before blessed darkness overtook me.

It was the same surreal dream, the same otherworldly garden. I sprawled on my back, nestled among dewy blades of grass, while he sat to my side on a low rattan stool. My older clone; his one leg folded over the other, his fist propping his chin, and his finger tapping his lips.

He watched me curiously, mouthing words that escaped me since the jackhammer inside my head hadn't quieted. *Brothers? Whose?* My limbs were heavy; immovable boulders pinning me to the grass, sinking me into the soil. And yet his mouth kept spouting inaudible speech, his eyes twinkling with mischief.

Then I came to, spread-eagled on my tummy and munching on gravel, a deathly hush shrouding every sign of life. I rolled onto my back and the street was intact: no smoldering cinders choking the air, no hills of chalky slag clouding my view.

I wasn't lucid for long, but for the lick of time my eyelids pried open, I could've sworn Chacha Kakakhel returned to the scene of violence. He sat on his haunches, inspecting the dud missile that'd defiled the road. Even in my catatonic state, his behavior struck me as most strange.

The geezer's knuckle purposely rapped its egg-white shell, and he fidgeted with its tailed fins. And while his shades now hung from his waistcoat pocket, my five o'clock position concealed his peepers. But I confess, never since have I seen such dexterity from a supposed blind man.

For a wasted second my thoughts strayed to Afi and his thugs, but I struggled to focus beyond Chacha and that was enough to soothe my conscience.

Hah, why ought I care a gnat's tush? I was keeping away from trouble until the gorilla baited me into a duel.

My eyelids again grew heavy, and I blacked out. Not until nightfall did, I stir next, when a battery of strobe lights broke my swoon. Ahead, near the crater, parked a boxlike ambulance and a trio of skinny cop bikes, while frenzied voices peaked over the crackle of wireless radio.

Chacha had disappeared, and in his place, a weaselly man sporting a broadsword mustache stood center stage in the commotion. Under the flickering streetlamp, he kept patting his sticky forehead and brushing his starchy kameez with tremulous hands.

I knew the guy; remembered him from months earlier when his smiley election posters filled the town walls. Ikhlaq, the reigning councilor and Afi's father. He'd inherited the top seat in Naya Chooran from his dad and gramps, God bless democracy.

My joints creaking, I rose onto all-fours and stealthily padded upslope to beyond the radiant corona of the strobes. As far as I cared, they could shack up in hell together. What skin did I, a cheap candy seller, have in this game? Who'd inquire my opinion if Naya Chooran went to war, or if the world ended? I needed only change my route until things settled and scram if the geezer again crossed my path.

Upon reaching the brushy junction, I straightened to my feet and staggered the distance home, planning to climb over our short boundary wall and curl up in the scarcely paved courtyard till dawn. But to my dismay, mother was waiting by our crooked gate, lantern in hand, fanning herself with a folded newspaper.

She'd plainly spent the day prepping her acid-dipped sermon, and wastefulness was not in her nature. In fact, only when she grilled me over the candy did I realize my basket still placed on the shop steps. Stupid, stupid. Her expert welting that night hurt far less than the renewed risk of running into Afi or Chacha.

Come morning, I strode toward the street, wincing while I kneaded my sore back, until the junction arrived and at once I halted. Something was amiss. Inside, a sea of people ebbed and flowed as an aimless concerto; their elbows and shoulders knocking together. A smattering of cops in seaweed green togs ringed them, their demeanors unusually tense, their brows furrowed.

Deeper still, a bullhorn squawked and crackled; a man's voice bellowing charged slogans I heard every Independence Day. The easterly enemy, this. The easterly enemy, that. Still, the cuckoos in the throng didn't care, their passionate chants turning the neighborhood into an echo chamber.

Well, whatever cause so animated them was none of my beeswax. These people excited over the dumbest things to fill their empty lives. Hell, they'd be boiling grass for dinner, yet thrill over the neighbors cooking mutton curry. And whenever their corrupt cricket team lost a game, they smashed the television sets they'd bought on borrowed money. Utter, blithering idiots, I tell you.

My goal was the shop stuck with the for-sale sign beside the lamppost bearing a maple leaf scar. I crept into the crowd, deftly snaking past gossiping aunties in gaudy prints and store owners grumping over lost sales, only to whack into a wall of fat and recoil.

The owner of said wall, the cop dwarfing me, wore the fish-eyed look of a man who'd just met Satan. His sticky hair matted under his aslant berry-blue beret, and his overhanging belly spasmed as a hummingbird on crack.

The police officer was fiddling with the top button of his collared shirt and biting on his bottom lip. His badge read: Bonga. "Watch where you're going," he said in a hoarse, unsteady voice.

Even as he scowled at me, often his gaze darted to the heavens, as though he were Chicken Little fretting a satellite could crash on his head.

The lamppost set a mere stone's throw away. My face formed a sheepish grin and my hands clasped together in a praying pose. "Sorry, *sirkar*. I'll be more careful next time."

Then I goose-stepped to the side, aiming to slip past him, when his hairy paw landed on my shoulder. Constable Bonga surveyed me suspiciously, the dark saucers under his eyes creasing. "What're you up to, huh?"

"Nothing, sirkar," I said, my stare glued to the lamppost. "I sell candies and left my basket here yesterday."

No sooner did those words leave my mouth that I swore under my breath. A dumb confession, given the circumstances. Argh, I should've learned from father how to lie convincingly.

Bonga leaned into me, grunting. "Yesterday, huh? What do you know about the incident?"

My gut knotted into a wrung dishcloth. "Not a thing, I swear. I just sell candy," I said, squirming to free myself of his clutches.

His eyes grew crazy. "You must be the bomber, yes? Here to gloat at our anguish. Admit it, goddamn you," he said, again and again jerking me as a rag doll.

The throng thickened round the lamppost while I ground my teeth to endure his intense BO, the bullhorn's amplified squall now punching holes in my brain. How soon before someone found my candies and lifted them?

The maze dwellers, I knew from experience, never fussed over the ownership of snacks that weren't theirs. Then the boneheads wondered why Allah favored the councilor and his ilk.

I had but one way to lose this madman. Preying on the insecurities of others was more mother's style, but no choice. My head tipped skyward for a beat, and then I looked him in the eye, horror-struck. "Another one's coming."

Bonga unhanded me pronto, stumbling backward into a circle of preppy rowdies who were busy battle-rapping in their own twisted corner of reality. Cussing, they whipped out their switchblades, and right away I sank into a crouch and started crawling through the crowd's legs.

But when I emerged breathless, the store steps littered with crumpled juice cartons but no basket. The high-voltage atmosphere then swallowed my fist-shaking screams. For this egregious flub, mother could nail me to the neem tree beside our gate.

That's when it hit me that without meaning to, I'd arrived at the heart of the action. Behind the towering dam of turned backs, a spirited voice barked through the bullhorn. Councilor Ikhlaq?

"Have no fear," it said. "We will bring the enemy to his knees."

Desperation overcame my better instincts. If it was our dear leader, I'd beg him to buy me a new wicker basket and two packs of cheap candies. Surely, he'd pity a fatherless urchin? Though beset by a cauldron of social ills, charity indeed was Naya Chooran's only saving grace.

Then I was wriggling through the crush, stamping on

countless sandaled feet and muttering a million pardons. While most forgave, I remember my cheeks stung from round half a dozen slaps.

And then I sighted him: bullhorn to lips, Ikhlaq stood behind the cone-shaped shell that still poked out the asphalt. Two burly cops and a faux-hawked midget with a pointy goatee flanked him, their features stony. Afi too lingered by his side; ramrod in his carriage and comically solemn.

My face scrunched up in chagrin. Did the rotten always escape death because Allah didn't want them returning in a hurry? Just once I'd love to see divine justice delivered. Yes, maybe a holy inferno razing the hillside, forcing the rich to flee downslope and cook their meals over sulfurous open fires while their pampered skins coated with soot.

"We're peace-loving folk," Ikhlaq said. "But if war comes to our backyard, we will meet it with valor and vanquish our foes. Naya Chooran zindabad!"

The crowd's first tiers threw up their fists and shouted an ear-splitting huzzah. And then it sounded again, leftward, that insane laugh that crossed a whistling train with a honking seal.

TAK-TAKA-TAK-TAKA-TAK. BALE-BALE!

Once more, raucous dhol beats and Punjabi hollers rang through the street.

The audience parted on cue, rubbernecking behind them to spot the culprit. Chacha, his aviators back on the nose, breached their ranks and gaily waved at the councilor.

Then the boom box silenced, and his face bore a simper. "Excuse me, sirkar, but who's the enemy?"

The midget stepped forward, harrumphing and checking his regimental necktie. "Our easterly neighbor, who else?"

"Oh, cat got the boss's tongue?"

"Councilor Ikhlaq can't hear too well," he said, his eyes squinching. "I'm his assistant, Kubba. Now don't interrupt, *baba-ji*. We're talking national security."

Chacha's shoulders shimmied in sync with his snickers. "So, the deaf leading the blind, eh?"

Murmurs buzzed round me as an angry beehive. Ikhlaq wore a quizzical look, his gaze flitting between Kubba and the crowd, but Afi had flushed a fierce red.

"This man is an enemy agent, I just know it," he yelled, his finger jabbing at Chacha. "He's the one who brought down the bomb."

Kubba glanced at the gorilla, and then he toyed with his precise goatee, his expression bleak. "Why would the boy accuse you, baba-ji?"

Chacha snorted, dismissively flapping his wrist. "You dimwits couldn't win a jug of *lassi*, much less the war that's coming. The easterly neighbor, you say. What hogwash!"

I face-palmed, a groan leaving my lips. Shit, shit, shit. The geezer's gone and stuck a wrench deep in their pride. And here I planned to invoke the councilor's sense of duty so he'd part with his cash. No choice, I'd have to panhandle for another basket.

The cops were inching toward Chacha, reaching for their pistol holsters, when Kubba held out an arm. Then his curled finger gestured to Ikhlaq, who stooped so the midget could speak into his ear.

His chatter was in a tongue unknown to me: a quick-fire string of clicks, clucks and drawly syllables. Those around me were scratching their scalps, perplexed, but not the councilor, nor indeed Chacha who kept his stolid demeanor.

Ikhlaq's lips pursed once Kubba finished, and he shot the geezer a nasty look. "Now listen here, baba-ji. Shut up unless you want to get jailed. This is a very serious situation."

Their testy exchange fired up my curiosity. Why'd Naya Chooran gain a new foe? They couldn't covet our doughy snuff that resembled dog poop.

I slipped beyond the vanguard and eyed Chacha. "Who's the villain, then? Who lobbed the shell yesterday?"

He hesitated, somewhat stunned, as if he were noticing me for the first time. "Why, the brothers Yajuj and Majuj," he said, showing a toothy smile.

The crowd gasped as one, and those in his vicinity unwittingly backed away. Yet elation surged through me, my clone's pantomime of speech flashing before my eyes. Was the dream then a warning?

Kubba's mood soured, and he shouted for order, his arms flailing overhead. "Now you've done it," he told Chacha when fussily beckoning the cops. "Get this fool out of here. Book him for public disorder without bail."

The police officers nodded grimly, tugging at their wide-buckled belts, and then they stormed toward the geezer. Unruffled, Chacha reached inside his waistcoat, to which they paused and unclipped their holsters.

He produced a curved horn the size of a fanny pack; stained porcelain bone, a silver mouthpiece; and raised it for everyone to see. "You know this magnificent thing?"

"A memento from your circus act?" Afi spat, now peeping from behind his father's back.

Chacha chuckled, wagging its pointy end in his direction. "No, son. This is what'll save your sorry behinds, if you agree to my condition, that is."

Kubba rushed to the stiff cop nearest him, whipped out his pistol, and promptly trained it at the geezer. "Screw this, I'll shoot you myself. Traitors like you will never roam scot-free on my watch."

A panicked whoop rose in the audience, and straightaway I cowered, glimpsing round for a quick exit. I'd heard enough. Pistols drawn in this town always meant accidental deaths and zero culpability. But my neighbors, ever the idle busybodies, squeezed together and made it impossible for me to steal away.

The lane fell into a funereal silence, and Chacha's arms raised in surrender. "You twerps act like you own this place. This is God's country."

"Oh, here on Allah's behalf, then?" Kubba asked, sneering.

"I've always done the Lord's work."

"Wow, you're one crazy old man."

Chacha noisily sighed, and snapping off his shades, he ambled toward Kubba. Though I couldn't tell from my position, whatever lay behind them blanched the midget's features.

The geezer looked to the sky and flicked the crest of his perky turban. "Another one's coming," he said, replacing his specs. "A live one."

A clicking sound when Kubba cocked the pistol. "Y-you. W-what do you want?"

"You should've read the inscription on the fins. Soon, it'll be too late."

"WHAT DO YOU WANT?" Ikhlaq repeated, panicked at his aide's pop-eyes.

"If you value your lives, make me your councilor right now."

Afi and Ikhlaq leaped away, yelping, when Chacha moseyed past the stupefied midget and toward the missile.

There, a large trash sack pulled out from under his vest, and he pinched the shell out of the crater; drew it with the ease of a toy buried in mud.

Blood retreated from my limbs, and I slumped onto the road, my eyes glued to his figure. What sorcery was this? Who was the geezer?

Chacha plonked the shell inside his sack that strangely made no sound, and again he peered heavenward. "I cannot abandon you as my sons did me. No, I cannot. I must cleanse you."

Then the bag pitched over his shoulder, and his thumb was flicking in my direction. "When you chumps come to your senses, ask this kid to call me. His name, as you know it, is Kalia. Remember well."

Sweat misted over my forehead as countless stares cored into my back. Why? Why was he pulling me into his lunacy?

The whine from yesterday returned; louder, more sinister.

And the white spot. It grew bigger and bigger through the blanket of dried milk-thick dust.

The crowd was stampeding, their shrieks bone-chilling.

I coiled into a fetal position on the blacktop, bracing my skull, gritting my teeth. If I survived the day, I swore I'd sew Chacha into a pincushion.

Chapter Three

The Mute Boy Who Spoke

"Run, fools," Kubba screeched, right before the ground shook and threw me into a somersault. Was Afi bawling or was it Councilor Ikhlaq? Or a street dog? Hysteria sounds so similar across species, ya know?

Chacha Kakakhel's scratchy tones cut through the cacophony. Twice he shouted, "remember, Kalia," before his voice melted into the slipstream of feral shrieks. And each time he said it, my heart plunged further, making a beeline for my bowels.

I feared for my life, and not just because the stampeders in their haste to flee banged against my spine and booted my posterior. Chacha, the idiot, may as well have broadcast my alleged complicity on national radio, and as the midget warned, they didn't take kindly to traitors round these parts.

Wild, wild anarchy everywhere. Soon the frenzied horde had turned the sandy lane into a swirling shower of grit and gravel. I couldn't see beyond the ends of my toes, which in hindsight was a blessing. I daren't commit more gruesome images to memory, for as a career street urchin, I'd effortlessly amassed a vast catalog of tragic experiences.

I was flat on my back, every morsel of my being benumbed, peeking through my shivering fingers at the missile diving toward the asphalt. Even if I binge-watched slasher flicks for the rest of my life, my frights couldn't approach the dread seizing me in that sliver of time. For in that moment, neither my basket, nor my mother, nor my destiny concerned me.

The next thing I knew, their clamor grew distant, and I was hovering high above the street, peering through blurry binoculars at my corporeal self still cringing on the road. Was I even conscious?

Then they loomed before me: two moonlike irises shimmering as an oil slick. Briefly, they tore into my soul, scouring through my memories that ran as a show-reel, before swapping for a photo album whose browning, grungy pages flipped on their own.

Each page held Polaroid snaps; photos of cavernous halls lined with colossal statues, of Moorish fortresses on barren mountaintops: empty, abandoned, caked in forbidding clay. What was this? The future or a bygone age? The album slammed shut asudden, curled up into parchment, and dissolved into dust.

An electric jolt, and I returned to my back, concussed. Wherever the stampeders were, they'd stopped screaming, and the sandstorm too had died. I inched upright and scrubbed the sand off my face.

What just happened? Where was I?

The missile was a live one alright, but not in the way anyone expected. With supernatural accuracy, it crashed into the rift whence Chacha had uprooted its forebear.

But the shell didn't go kaboom and smash us into a blood-and-guts chapati. Instead, it kept sizzling as a firecracker, whiffing sharp rings of smoke, and then it snuffed out and went silent. Those excruciating minutes, I tell you, could've driven a snail to suicide.

While it behooved me to escape, my limbs refused to abide, even as I furiously kneaded them to get the blood flowing. Another dud? Was the enemy a complete moron? Or toying with us as a sadistic cat does a trapped cockroach? I praised Allah for leaving me whole, but the gratitude didn't last long. It never did.

Disembodied hands, tough and vinelike, grabbed my shoulders from behind and yanked me erect. Then a coarse fabric tightly wrapped over my eyes, and a thick wad of paper stuffed into my mouth.

The goons didn't need to blindfold or drug me with chloroform, for resistance in my condition was futile. At the time I couldn't coax my parched throat to croak, much less thrash my arms or holler for help.

And so, I limped alongside them, their stringless puppet, until the men shoved me into a vehicle, a van I presumed from the swoosh of a sliding door. The van's shallow seat wore its padding wafer-slim, which ached my tush as though I'd slept the night on a tombstone.

In my trancelike state, it was hard to guess how long the vehicle bumped and clattered round town, but an hour must've passed before I understood they'd tossed me into a dank windowless cell that stank of mothballs and sour milk. And another before I stopped shouting myself hoarse while rattling its steel bars.

Beyond the bars, the bare arena held the aura of a torture chamber; lit by rows of halogen bulbs dangling from the low ceiling that cast long shadows inside my cell. Over its slick floor displayed a gather of vacant office desks, and behind them on the stark wall nailed a giant blackboard chalked with names and numbers in scrawly longhand. And besides the cheeping and hustling of shadowy rats, the place was a graveyard. An echoey graveyard.

In my brief life, I'd never felt so weary as when I dumped onto the cell's stony floor, tucked in my knees, and cradled my head atop my locked arms. What to do? Even if she knew, mother wasn't coming to free me. Given her stable of dependable scammers, could you blame her? Doubtless she was glad there'd be more sleeping space for the useful brood, and now they could upgrade dinner from watery gruel to veggie curry.

That's when he mumbled and scared the daymares out of me: a puny boy round my age, huddled up in the far corner as an empty mailbag. I'd slipped off my scissor slipper and held it swordlike at my chest when I met his guileless stare.

Though he too dressed in a threadbare salwar kameez, his baby-faced, bright-eyed demeanor belied his plight. Well, they'd jailed me without fault too. God bless Naya Chooran, home of the bobbleheads.

The kid sat up, busily dabbing his mussy hair, grinning at me; that sweet, eyes-shrunk-to-slits grin you saw in Japanese cartoons. They were cute, those cartoons. Sometimes I'd consciously catch my breath outside the chai shop where the owner's children were always watching dubbed versions of them. They sprang a strange yearning in me, as if I'd missed meaningful chunks of childhood.

I took in a lungful to compose myself and replaced my slipper. His company wasn't unwelcome given my plight. "What're you doing here?"

The boy briskly nodded, letting loose a flurry of hand signs that startled me, but not because he couldn't speak. Hell, I'd seen enough mangled limbs to fill a medical encyclopedia. What struck me was the vivid artistry of his movements, akin to a hobo Bruce Lee.

My jaw shut, and I shook my head. "Don't understand you. What's your name? Can you trace it on the floor?"

Once more he nodded, and his remarkably curved fingernail began sketching letters over the concrete. His speed slowed each instance, and throughout he threw me inquisitive looks.

Good thing I'd stayed in school long enough to learn the alphabet. Had a genuine talent for language too, my teachers said. They'd marvel at my imagination, those tales of yore I effortlessly conjured, as if they sprang from deep within me.

I'd tried storytelling at street corners to sell kids more candy, even reenacted scenes to spice up the good bits, but the young ones round town, I concluded, couldn't think beyond their tummies.

M-u-j-i. "Muji?" I asked.

Beaming, he shot me a thumbs-up, and then gestured for mine

"They call me Kalia," I said, slouching against the flaky wall. "That's more an insult, I know, but I got no clue about my birth name."

Muji's unceasing gaze creeped me, and I turned my attention to the empty desks. Argh, how to locate Chacha? The geezer landed me in this mess and only he could acquit me. And tell me my actual name, he'd hinted as much. I hated introducing myself as Kalia; I'd never even call my pooch that. Stupid, or owl-spawn, sounded much better.

CLANG-CLANG-CLANG. The cell bars clanged as a thunderclap, and I flinched.

Past them stood Bonga, the paranoid cop from earlier. He was glaring at me, a thick baton beating into his cupped palm. He'd traded his police togs for a khaki uniform, and on his dark armband stitched a strange military crest.

"I knew you were trouble the moment I saw you," Bonga said. Then he sighted Muji and frowned. "Who's that boy?"

I shot to my feet, my nostrils flaring, my balled fists quivering at my sides. "Why did you jail me, officer?"

He fired me the look of death. "That's Captain Bonga, pip-squeak. The new Naya Chooran paramilitaries."

My lips twisted in bafflement. "Huh? The army's not here yet?"

Bonga's jowls flushed for a flicker. "We don't need no army," he said, thumping his chest. "Our brave men will defend this land."

I curbed a sarcastic grunt. Yea, him and the braves who'd nearly soiled their pants over a failed bomb. "Splendid. Now free me."

The baton whanged the bars anew, and his stink eye revived. "Who're you and what's the old fogy scheming?"

Both excellent questions, to which I had no answers. Just my luck, this imbecile believed I was in league with the geezer.

I doubled over and clutched my knees, sighing. "I swear on the Koran, I don't know."

Bonga kept his scowl. "Think you're tough, huh? You wait, I'll have you singing nursery rhymes in no time."

I gave him a tired look, but kept silent. His kind could make me disappear without a trace. Such disappearances happened daily in this town, even if news channels never reported them. Well, what of it? Poverty had always kept me invisible.

Muji was following our testy back-and-forth with great interest, his razor-edged fingernail tapping the floor as a telegraph operator.

Bonga's peepers now fixed solely on Muji, his brow knitted. "Goddammit, who's that kid?" From his breast pocket he drew a slim notepad and was flipping through its pages.

I glowered at him; my fingers set on my skinny hips. Mistaking me for a criminal was one thing, but jailing a mute child without cause should be punishable by death. "You don't know why he's here?"

The cop clawed at his chest; his plump lips puckered in confusion. Then Muji shot up a hand and was bouncing on his rump. Then he mumbled anew, unleashing another volley of signals.

I cast the lad a sad smile. Does he think the big lug will cut him any slack? Poor sap, he must be new to town. "He can't speak, *kaptan* sirkar."

The cop ignored me, the whites of his eyes widening. "You can help?" he asked Muji. "How?"

My jaw slackened at his question. "What? You get him?"

The kid kept at his kung-fu while Bonga scribbled on the pad, now and again gasping. "Locate the next missile? No kidding."

Then he turned to me, squinting. "You and your buddy

here better not be playing me. I can declare you enemy agents anytime and order a firing squad."

"He's not my buddy," I protested.

"Locked up together, aren't you?" asked Bonga, smirking, his pen knocking on the pad. "My report distinctly states he's your accomplice."

My arms threw up in exasperation. "Does it also say you're brainless?"

Bonga's pinkies stuck between his lips, and he blew out a shrill whistle that rang through the hall. Soon, two uniformed men marched up to him and saluted.

"Time's a wasting. Let's get you traitors to work," he said, keying open the cell door.

Straightaway, his po-faced deputies barged inside and were manhandling me to the exit. My legs flailed for dear life, my neck straining sideways so I could bite their arms. "I got nothing to do with this. Lemme go."

Muji came to my side and touched my shoulder, his countenance reassuring, and yet a chill swept through me, though my brain couldn't compute why. Then he strolled out ahead, stretching his limbs as a boy scout ready to peg tents. Was he used to captivity?

We shoved along a lonely corridor aglow with the same halogen bulbs and scented with a strong antiseptic. That we were underground only hit me once we boarded an old-school elevator with cage-style gates, which climbed through a tunnel marked with buzzing orange lamps and swayed so much I was seasick.

There was no point reasoning with Bonga or his underlings, I decided. I'd have to take my chances with his superiors, though whoever promoted the crackpot to captain was just as insane.

Before long, the elevator squeakily braked and thudded to a stop. Bonga's henchmen at once drew back the gates and reached for a creaky shutter with rounded slats. At first, I shaded my eyes, wincing at the outbreak of light, but then my breath hitched.

We'd returned to the street, that damn street. It was eerily quiet but for the whispering of a sooty breeze. Kubba beckoned us from the blast site around twenty feet away, his expression glum. It was plain only Chacha could extract the shells.

And below the steps stood the lamppost with the maple leaf scar. I swallowed hard, my heart playing hopscotch inside my ribs. How was that possible?

Muji clapped with glee, and he toddled toward the road with us in pursuit. My hand outstretched to graze the scar, the memory of my lost basket and what it wrought twingeing my gut.

Bonga and his lackeys threw their shoulders back and saluted Kubba, and then they thrust us toward him.

"Hey, you've made a big mistake," I said, recovering my balance.

The gnome paid me no mind. "Any word from the army?"

"They're not taking this seriously, sir," said Bonga. "They have no report of an attack, nothing on their radars."

Kubba's head dipped, and he silently pinched his squat nose. Then he motioned toward the missile, growling. "Does this look like an albino pumpkin?"

I stepped toward him, furiously waving my arms. "Sirkar, listen to me!"

Kubba caressed the bulge over his jacket shaped as a firearm. "Go drum up recruits," he told Bonga. "I'll deal with these two."

Once more my mouth dried into a drought. Take off at first chance, Kalia. I should outrun him easily and jump a wall, any wall. Stay low till night came. Shit, but what if he was a reasonable shot? Risky, too risky. I couldn't zig and zag; I wasn't a ninja. Argh, if only I were a djinn or possessed a magic carpet.

Muji, meanwhile, was glancing round the lane as if he were a weekend tourist lazing in a theme park. Or someone who'd emerged from the underworld after a long repose. I suppose he was both.

The midget peered skyward and heaved a sigh. "How can you chumps help me? Don't take all day now."

"I can't," I said in a cracking voice.

Kubba was unmoved. "How do we nab the old man?"

"I don't even know who the hell he is."

His face distorted from anger, and a snarl left his lips. "Quit lying, twerp. Okay, where's the next hit?"

I raised on my tiptoes; my fists cocked at my hips. "If I had such foresight, you think I'd be selling cheap candy round town?"

Then Muji drew the midget's attention by spouting a strange cocktail of speech; clicks, clucks, and drawled syllables.

I shot him a surprised look, since he sounded as a cranky rooster quarreling with a wowing cassette player. And yet oddly familiar, as when Kubba spoke in Ikhlaq's ear.

The midget approached Muji, thunderstruck. "You know where? Who are you?"

The boy showed a smug grin, and onward he chattered in the alien tongue.

Kubba grabbed a fistful of his faux-hawk. "I see, I see. Must inform the councilor ASAP."

"What's he saying?" I asked, incredulous, but they ignored my interjection.

Muji's forefinger raised to cut an invisible circle overhead, to which Kubba swore while jiggling his chunky jeweled rings. "Y-yes. We need help," he said.

But the boy's wrist flapped in dissent, and from his pocket he pulled out a tooth-cleaning *miswak* stick, which he flourished as a wand while gibbering without pause.

Kubba attended to him, bewitched. "True, sacrifices are necessary to bring down the brute."

Their stares together fixed on me, their features sunless and stony.

Porcupine quills were needling my chest. To my mind, I'd leave the second I convinced Kubba of my innocence, but now I found myself dragged into the twilight zone.

Kubba coughed into his fist and neared me. "You want to help us win the war, correct?"

Argh, I should've known the pocket-sized sneak was a master manipulator. He knew I wanted my life back, yet expressing such was unmanly. Call it brainwashing or whatever, but patriotism and manhood were synonymous in Naya Chooran.

And thus, I idiotically puffed out my chest. "Zindabad."

A faint smile crossed Kubba's lips when he slipped out his pistol and trained the barrel at me. "Good, then we'll need you to stay underground for now."

I backpedaled on instinct. "Y-you're imprisoning me again?"

"The director thinks its best that way," he said, stealing a glance at Muji.

"Huh? What director?"

The boy eyed me blankly, and then he was wandering up the road, humming and swishing his stick as if counting ghosty sheep.

An arctic frost seized me, the sense of drowning in icy water. Where was Chacha Kakakhel? Why'd he forsaken me? Was I destined to perish underground, more fodder to fatten those infernal rats?

When Kubba led me back up the shop steps, his pistol digging into my spine, I prayed the geezer was alive so I could bury him personally.

— Chapter Four —

Heroes and Weasels

How many days now? Three? A week? I'd lost count since the diabolical midget, may Allah smite him, again confined me underground.

My waking hours I spent pacing the cell or picking lice from my scalp, again and again replaying the scenes from that afternoon, yet emerging none the wiser. The rats scurried round me unconcerned; coming and going as they pleased, nibbling on my neck and ears, indifferent to my yelps and scoldings.

Occasionally I mumbled snatches of song, but there weren't many lyrics I remembered. Pity. My fellow urchins were always belting out popular ditties, saying it made their toil bearable, and that I was a weirdo for dwelling over unnecessary things. I'd scoff at their answer. The fools didn't realize men bore their burdens without band-aids.

Recalling that traitor Muji gave me daily migraines. Hah, I should've known better than to trust people who showed me an ounce of kindness, who didn't scorn me as if I were an ingrown toenail. Maybe mother was right. She believed humans were horrid creatures, especially her husband. If only I'd paid more attention between the beatings and not merely wished we were galaxies apart.

Often, I fantasized of offing Chacha in the most gruesome ways. Murder didn't come naturally to me, but the geezer made a compelling case. I'd rethink my opinion if he soon came to my rescue, but failing that, I'd fast-forward his trip to the coffin.

A djinn or warlock he may be, but I'd find a way. In Allah I trusted and surely he'd deliver me. It's not as if the big guy was busy changing lives or bettering the world, at least not Naya Chooran.

Whenever I awoke, a dented metal tray unfailingly set beside the cell door. Bless the fiends for small favors, but the holidaying rats often got to the papery flatbread first, so I'd sip on soggy *dhal* and comfort my grumbling tummy. Many people in town, I argued with my gut, could kill for my slim pickings.

My repose was as restless as a bookie who'd backed the wrong bird in a cockfight. Most kids my age dreamed wondrous dreams; of playing superheroes or celebrities, of grand adventures and grander treasures.

Me, of late, I only dreamed the surreal. As if meeting my cryptic clone wasn't enough, my mind had crafted another absurd chimera.

That dream always started with an inky whirlpool, unending. No beginning, no end. It drew me inside and I couldn't resist. Deeper and deeper I sank in its spirals while it roared round me, smelling of saltwater and samosas.

Sometimes the roars relented, and I sensed snippets of music, and ghostly whispers, and the clashing of steel. Then came cracks of thunder, a pattering drizzle, cries of joy. I was there, yet I wasn't. Who was I? Why was I? Who do I ask these questions?

I was gossamer, floating aimlessly in a monstrous storm's eye. The voices, I assumed, were embers of events past, infinitely more significant than I'd ever be, but that didn't concern me. I learned long ago the sweeping strokes of the human experience mattered little to my kind. Wait, why did I believe that?

Each time the episode ended with a brilliant light rising from the whirlpool's bowels and enwrapping me. It fired electric bolts through my body and I'd revive soon after, panting heavily and perspiring as though I were a cast-iron kettle.

But that day was special. The radiance did not devour me and instead made many flaming orbs that circled before my eyes: slaves to a celestial juggler.

The air seethed and sizzled as their violent dance grew faster and faster until my skin pruned and blistered and oozed black blood. I was howling in agony, louder and louder, until the globes smashed together and collapsed into nothingness.

And then someone flipped on the floodlights.

I cussed, covering my face until his infuriating laugh pricked my ears. On instinct I lunged forward, my fists shaped into claws, ready to choke him lifeless.

But my rage forthwith swapped for fear when I nearly fell off my high-legged stool that hovered in midair. Round ten feet away, Chacha Kakakhel too floated on the same seat wearing a slaphappy expression.

Around us lay an outfield of dazzling emerald green, fenced by spired grandstands that sparkled as princely manors. And beside the monotonic hum of the light towers and Chacha's chronic wheezing, the place was soundless. We were floating over a glassy pitch in the world's loneliest cricket stadium. No chirping grasshoppers or pesky gnats, no dragging feet or idle chatter. No life.

Such a farce was unthinkable unless a mortal pandemic shut humankind indoors. Well, the moneybags in Naya Chooran for sure deserved the punishment.

Chacha was coolly picking his nose; his attire unchanged, beside the curved horn that strung round his collar as a protective charm. Mercifully, his annoying boom box was missing. "How goes it, son?"

My fingers clutched the seat plank tighter while I glared at him. "What'd I ever do to you, huh?"

He made a serious face and scratched his temple. "I didn't expect you to show up either, you know. Threw my plans all awry."

"Make sense, goddammit."

For an instant Chacha's wispy brow hiked, and then he sighed. "You're still Kalia. No wonder it took so long."

I mopped my forehead in exasperation and blew out a noisy breath. "What did? Forget it. Just clear my name and I swear I'll keep away from whatever you're scheming."

Chacha shook his head. "Sorry, kid. Wish there were another way. We need you or history will repeat itself."

Was the geezer duping me again? "Is that why you told them only I could reach you? And then disappeared?"

He shrugged, simpering. "I had no choice."

My arms folded over my chest while I pouted. If a meat cleaver were handy, I'd have diced him into a thousand ribbons sans remorse. Or fired up a super-sized cannon and have him go kablooey. I'd even have settled for remodeling his face with my slipper. If only I were as my doppelganger, tall and strapping, without delay I'd whisk him into an omelet.

Chacha perked up, tipping forward on his stool. "You're a man, right? What makes one?"

"To act as one, what else?" I said, flourishing my finger. "A man's word should be unshakable."

He rubbed his palms, nodding in agreement. "Great, so let's make a deal? A pact between men. You help me, I help you."

I drummed my knees, my eyes narrowing. "You've proven more of a weasel to date."

Chacha swatted away my concern. "Fair enough, we'll start over," he said, tapping the rim of his shades. "Guess why I wear these."

I recalled him examining the missile, and then Kubba's ashen face when he removed the aviators. "You're not blind, are you?"

Chacha shushed me, placing a finger to his lips that formed a raffish smile. "This is top, top secret, but you have to know. No changing that."

Then he reached for his specs, his head pitching a few degrees, and my heart ba-dumped. Was he a cyclops? Or a zombie with bloodshot eyes? No, he must have lasers for pupils, the kind that could incinerate buildings.

The next thing I knew, Chacha made the teapot pose, his brow flashing high and low. "Really something, eh?"

I jerked backward on the stool, a shriek catching in my throat. How could this be? Was I dreaming inside the dream?

Behind his shades, above the nose, churned a black hole rippling in a clockwise motion: the inky whirlpool that'd haunted me for days. No eye sockets, only an abyss.

Chacha stuck on his glasses. "The cover still won't fit," he said, patting the horn. "But that's life for you."

I didn't respond. I couldn't respond. Not in my darkest fantasy could I evoke a beast as him. Yep, getting even was futile. The geezer ignored my gawking and beamed as though I'd just petted his baby giraffe.

"You've met my little brother, yes? Now that guy is the sneakiest fellow I know," he said, snickering.

Over and over I swallowed, quelling the urge to slap myself to sanity. It must be that knave, Muji. Nothing else made sense since Bonga's sibling could only be a baboon. "K-kubba and the councilor. Who are they?"

"Oh, you noticed? Clever boy," said Chacha, glowing as a proud parent.

Right then something snapped in me, my terror spilling over into outrage. Argh, I was so done dancing to his tune, their tune. I slid off the stool, landing on the pitch in a crouch. "What do you want with me?"

Chacha arched backward, his fingers lacing behind his neck. "Aren't you the brave one after seeing my oculus?"

I shot upright and stomped on the hard loam, glowering. "Enough. You better start explaining or you can forget my help. Who are you people and who's warring with Naya Chooran?"

Chacha's palms bobbed to calm me. "Patience, my little friend. Time for an ancient story and don't get bored quickly. You may be the hero."

At the dawn of civilization, he began in a raspy voice, God tasked two brothers to wreak havoc on Earth. He didn't say why, and they didn't bother asking.

For centuries they rampaged the globe over, reducing entire nations to flaming rubble.

One brother sometimes acted as the savior, and once he'd baited the locals to trust him, they joined forces to unleash devastation and despair. Though the mind games weren't necessary, these kept them entertained.

The brothers were invincible and infinite in their lust for violence. One after another, they felled pharaohs, and false gods, and famed kings, but the Lord's angel warned them not to cross a particular river to the East. For centuries, the abundance of prey round them curbed their curiosity, but then they tired of easy kills and in their conceit defied God.

Across the river they met a youth, timid of carriage, the seventh son of the sultan of a kingdom bordering the banks. He greeted them as old friends, and his silver tongue convinced them he'd help overthrow his father if he could rule in his stead.

They agreed, seeing in young Zulkarnain a fellow evil, but he instantly forsook them. Wielding a supernatural gift unclear to Chacha, he stole the source of their power: their runic horn and staff, and forever banished them inside an impenetrable fortress.

As Chacha recounted the tale, my eyes glazed over, vivid snapshots of utter ruin flashing before them. A hillocky hand carved from fiery sand. One by one, it felled skyscraping towers and turned lush farmlands to pillowy dust. Shivers racked my body in tidal waves. Whose memories were these?

The geezer's chin pinched between his thumb and forefinger, and he wore a pensive look. "Thing is, I'm not sure who freed us."

My reverie cracked on a dime. "Huh?"

"Yajuj at your service," said Chacha, faking a bow.

I gaped at him, slumping onto the pitch. Muji-Muji-Majuj. Yajuj and Majuj, the demonic brothers of lore! How'd they escape their eternal prison? Wait, those surreal dreams. Was my doppelganger warning me of them?

"A-are you going to kill everyone?" I asked, hugging myself to stop the shudders.

"No, you nitwit," said Chacha, tsk-tsking. "We're no longer the superpowers of old. Why, even my brother could slay me as I am now. Anyway, I'm on your side."

The browning photo album popped up in my mind anew. Was it a record of their calamitous exploits? "Why?"

His features steeled. "There are beings protecting this land. Won't let us do our thing."

A hollow chuckle escaped me. "Naya Chooran? What's there to protect?"

"Great question," Chacha said, wagging his finger. "Only the big man upstairs knows, but these things, they're powerful. Scary, even."

The geezer's words should've comforted me, and to a degree they did, but likewise a disquiet opened in my gut. "Nothing to worry about then," I said, curling my toes.

"Wrong. They cannot defy the will of the people, so my brother is tricking them." Chacha's shoulders humped, and he heaved a sigh. "If only they'd made me councilor."

My lips shaped into an O. "You mean—"

"Yes. The missiles, they're his doing. And he lucked out since it appears the peasant class of our tribe did very well for themselves."

That unearthly language. "Kubba and Ikhlaq?"

Chacha touched his forehead, lightly shaking his head. "I told them to read the inscription on the shell. Our seal's right there on the fins. Those imbeciles have forgotten Majuj's guile."

Wow, how little I knew of Naya Chooran, and here I subscribed to every rumor-mill within city limits. But I couldn't shake the gnawing sensation in my solar plexus that an important piece to this puzzle was amiss. What was it?

I spread flat on my back, peering past the halo of the floodlights into the Stygian, starless sky. "You never explained why you're on our side."

A shuffling sound reached my ears. Chacha had dropped from his stool to sit cross-legged on the pristine rolled clay, his fingertips pressing together in a steady beat.

"After my sons helped Zulkarnain keep us captive, rage blinded me and I swore revenge on humanity," he began wistfully. "But years ago, when I scouted Naya Chooran, the guardians showed me the error of my ways."

"You seek redemption now, is that it?" I asked, snorting.

"No, son. I want to be a man. I want to do the right thing."

His past deeds merited no sympathy, and yet my heart squeezed and released. "Why me? Why not show yourself to the councilor and confess?"

"That'll do nothing," he said, his wrist waving fanlike. "You'll find this hard to believe, but you're Zulkarnain's offspring or his reincarnation. Otherwise, the whirlpool would've melted you into goop."

Another violent shiver struck me, and I snapped upright. "Liar. Me?"

"I'd hoped not, too," said Chacha with a wan smile. "But you have an unearthly aura, same as his."

He silently stroked his beard. "How the mighty have fallen, eh? I bet the forebears of your king cleaned horse poop in my time."

Should I celebrate or mourn? Me, the progeny of an immortal hero? The one who held the demonic duo at bay? That made no sense. Weird dreams aside, I was merely a street urchin now locked underground. His revelation raised no courage, no heroism in me. And yet it sparked a profound loathing. Why?

Chacha's finger snap caught my attention. "Dithering again, aren't you?" he asked in a deadpan.

My face screwed up in anger. "Easy for you to say. You're part demon."

He cleared his throat with the force of a champion loogie chucker. "True, true. But it's not all bleak. You have an ally on the outside."

"Oh! Who?" I asked, my spirits lifting.

Chacha shot me a disapproving look. "Don't get ahead of yourself. The most important thing is I become councilor as soon as possible."

I threw up my arms, annoyed. "You're like a jabbering mynah."

"You must understand," he said seriously. "These beings won't help us against Majuj until the people decide so. And we can't win without them."

My brain sputtered from his info dump, and I clasped my temples, groaning. Should I tell mother? She'd believe me, right? "Maybe I should just skip town."

"You could," said Chacha, his lips curling up as a sturgeon's. "But will that make you a man?"

My lips smacked in irritation. The infernal geezer knew

what buttons to push. "Fine, but I'm not dying for these ingrates. What has Naya Chooran ever done for me?"

He stared at me overlong and without comment. "Only you can answer that question."

Goddamn this guilt-tripping fogy. I got to my feet and brushed over my clothes. "What's the plan?"

"Majuj's staff," said Chacha brightly, his wrist polishing the horn. "Or something similar he keeps with him at all times. Steal it."

The miswak stick Muji brandished that day. "You think I can overpower his handlers, much less him? You're crazy."

His lips drew back, his chipped teeth glinting. "My brother has a fatal weakness. Your ally knows, or at least he should unless he's a total stooge."

The piano wire noosing round my throat relaxed. "That's something. Now, who is he?"

"Afi," he said, shooting me a victory sign.

My confidence emptied as a stung balloon. "You're really crazy."

Chacha hissed a laugh. "Well, I didn't deny the first time, did I?"

— Chapter Five —

Yajuj the Rat

I confess I'd met no one with Chacha Kakakhel's obscene sense of comedy. It was the kind you expected of someone aspiring for the electric chair, or a life sentence among famine-stricken cannibals.

Once he told me that pompous gorilla, Afi, was my only ally, I craved to put his smarmy mug to a blowtorch and feed his charred remains to the rebel warthogs who after midnight intruded upon town. Yes, he was part demon, indeed more formidable than his frail looks suggested, but no way I'd let him screw me over without conveying my extreme displeasure.

Alas, before I could properly express such, the stadium shattered as a brittle windowpane: its shards at first shimmering paper planes that sailed round the blackness before fading into a fleeting outburst of light.

Again, I was plunging through the coaly whirlpool, my mental compass going bonkers from the free-fall. I couldn't tell high from low; left from right.

In that moment I felt nothing but sheer futility; fitting, given my life's path to that point.

This time the whirlpool's waves moiled with superior vigor and reeked of fish, dead and bloated. My fingers reached out to skim them and they responded in kind, but I pulled back the instant they formed faces, gooey and grotesque.

How could the eddy so accurately recreate their features? Even as ghastly gelatin, mother's intense frown caught my breath; her slimy lips saying things I didn't want to hear. Father as usual was looking away, conversing with my smiley siblings.

Chacha's parting words kept pinging round my head. He'd announced, "all you need is love," and burst into fine mist, thus cutting short my torrent of choice swears. Argh, why couldn't the infuriating codger ever talk sense? For an ancient demon, he owned every bit the dignity of a bedwetting toddler.

I admonished Allah again for burdening me with unreasonable expectations. This acting-a-man business was dandy so long as I fended for myself, but I was supremely unfit to save others. Yet if I failed the mission, could I still call myself one? The Almighty never responded, though sometimes his sly laugh snuck into my heart and gave it a soul-wrenching shake.

The return trip took a far heavier toll on me, as if I were running a hundred-meter sprint saddled with a truckload of flour sacks. The waves cast an oppressive gravity that creaked my bones and swum my head, and before long, my chest was a twig caught in a typhoon, ready to snap into a million pieces.

Clickety-clack, clickety-clack: annoying as a grandfather's clock. And panting, so much panting. An entire pack of dogs?

Who called out my name? Metal groaned and grumped, and then a rustling sound. The cell door?

I rolled onto my side, drool eking out the rim of my lips, grumbling. Why couldn't people let me mope in peace? Detained against my will, and yet these busybodies insisted on ruining my snooze, the only time my troubles didn't absolutely crush me.

Pincerlike fingers dug into my shoulders, again and again jolting them, and then my backside twinged from a swift kick. I sat up, a freed horsewhip, and forthwith my noggin met an immovable object. A helmeted figure was staggering backward, holding his head, moaning.

"Ow," said Afi, throwing me a nasty look. "What's your problem, owl-spawn?"

Terrific, the clown had arrived. I'd need a leprechaun's luck to emerge from this mission unscathed. I rubbed my throbbing forehead and scowled. "You attack me and I'm the owl-spawn?"

Then I did a double take. "Why are you dressed like that?"

Afi squared his shoulders, cockily grinning, and threw me a crisp salute. "Major Afi, at your service."

Yes, a clown, the most ridiculous one I'd seen yet. Afi's sable turtleneck pulled low to his two-toned shorts, below which he sported high-collared combat boots. His bicycle helmet he'd spray-painted the shade of wheat and taped a crown of sprigs round its edges. And over his beefy chops, he'd smeared an avocado-green pigment that stank of kerosene.

An avalanche of mirth crested to my lips, and I should've exploded into laughter and unleashed a barrage of wisecracks, but my position demanded tact.

"How did you get here?" I asked, clambering to my feet.

Afi's arms fell limp to his sides, and he pouted. "I'm sure you meant to say thanks, Afi. I'm glad you came, Afi. You're a lifesaver, Afi."

"Go to hell, Afi."

For a beat, his face shone eggplant-purple and his lips quivered. Then his nose scrunched up and he spun toward the door. "Fine, rot in here forever," he said, lumbering away.

At once I swore under my breath. Kalia, you fool, the gorilla's your sole ticket out of this hellhole. "Wait, wait. Truce. We need to save Naya Chooran," I said, my hand reaching out in his direction.

Afi huffed back to me, and his finger over and over poked my ribs, "Let's get one thing straight, you little shit. I'm only here because I gave the geezer my word as a man."

I nodded along, fake earnest, while he launched into a lecture of his many virtues, none of which I believed. But the fact was Naya Chooran couldn't return to normal unless we foiled Majuj. Not that my town was remotely perfect, but it was the grim devil I knew.

Afi's grasp of the demon's weakness could be decisive, as long as we didn't need to track the tooth fairy or a seven-toed witch. Even if I'd been Zulkarnain in a past life, or was his progeny, my sole superpower was picking pockets in public buses.

"Yes, yes. I'm very grateful," I said for the hundredth time, simpering. "What's the plan?"

Surprise flickered on Afi's face. "Hey, aren't you curious how the brilliant me found you?"

A tired sigh escaped me. "That's the first question I asked."

He rolled his eyes and clucked. "You poor schmucks are all the same, so impatient."

I yanked my curls, fully intending to rip a fistful and stuff them into his stupid maw. For putting me through this, I ought to decapitate Chacha with a rusty saw. "Please tell."

Afi's trap opened and straightaway shut. Then his hands fastened to his hips and his brow cocked. "Wait, you never asked how I got my lofty rank."

I resisted the impulse to kick his crotch. "I did. First question."

Right away he perked up, lifting his finger in mock triumph. "Well done, well done."

Before I knew it, he was recapping in great detail the events from when the original missile fell, and the faint drip-dripping of water reached my ears. Must've been a leaky faucet somewhere round the dungeon, but naturally I'd never noticed because nothing had so bored me to tears. I should beg for Bonga's firing squad before the ape slew every one of my brain cells.

After what felt forever, Afi's arms outspread with pride. "And ta-da, that's how I made a major."

The pulsing in my forehead had revived with a vengeance. "Huh?" I asked, wincing.

He glowered at me. "Weren't you listening? I'm a major in the Naya Chooran revolutionary guard."

A shaft of euphoria stabbed through my gloom. Guard, as in plural? Other people willing to fight Muji? "No kidding, how many are we?"

Afi thumbed toward himself, smirking. "You have me, my dear fellow. Your one-man army."

The urge to barf grew overpowering. Did this moron fall on his head straight out of the womb? "Allah's wrath, did Chacha explain—"

"And I got here," Afi continued with sweeping hand gestures, "through ingenious spy work."

I crossed my arms, glaring at him. "Right. Where were the map and key? Under your pillow or up your tush?"

He blushed and limply flicked his wrist. "Oh, stop it."

"Listen, you dimwit," I said, pressing on my temples. "We have to steal Muji's miswak stick and make Chacha the councilor. That kid's been duping your dad and Kubba, not that it takes much."

Afi harrumphed and again saluted me, though this time with dimmed enthusiasm. "Understood. You're the ranking officer. We must save our town."

Then he leaned in, his hand cupping round the corner of his cavernous mouth. "Psst! Muji has a big weakness."

I arched away, pulling a face, the kerosene singeing my nostrils. "Why are you whispering? What is it?"

Afi's fist struck his flattened palm. "I'm not there yet. Thing is, he keeps sending roses and asking me to show him the sights. What super-villain does that?"

An unpleasant thought stirred in me, but I dismissed it outright, since no creature dead or alive could be that desperate. No way Chacha meant that. "What's he up to then?" I asked, unmoved.

He glimpsed over his shoulder and round the cell, squinty-eyed. "Muji helped the paramilitaries intercept new missiles. They made him director of defense; I think. He's a hero now."

A cartoon anvil set on my chest. So that's what Kubba meant. Not good, the demon had gained their trust too swiftly.

"Without a plan, we may as well bid Naya Chooran goodbye," I said, scratching the flaming itch on my chin.

Afi mimicked my pose and wore a thoughtful look, which I figured was only skin deep. Talking to him had convinced me he was nothing but bluster with wood shavings packed between his ears. Thus, the burden of strategy fell on me, which wasn't a comforting thought.

They didn't teach battling mythical monsters in any school I knew. Argh, why hadn't my clone reappeared? I needed a hint, any clue, no matter how cryptic. Damn him, why was he so whimsical? Must he behave precisely as me?

I exhaled a heavy breath. "Let's go, I need to scope the town. You used the elevator to get here?"

"Elevator?" asked Afi, blinking rapidly.

A woolly winter sock slipped out from his pocket; white with gray toes; and he held it toward me. "My instructions were to rub this thrice, and I'd reach you."

On the sock's instep, in lurid colors, stitched Chacha's grinning mug beside the message: *Naya Chooran or bust!*

My teeth gritted from fury. The rotten comedian could've created a secret passage to Muji's bedroom, or passed a talisman that weakened him long enough for us to swipe his stick. But oh no, to his feeble mind, a leg warmer sufficed. Next time, I ought to return the favor and sock his nose into a persimmon.

I slapped my cheeks twice and jiggled my arms loose. "Alright then."

Afi tightened his helmet strap, gulping. "Hang on, I can't get used to this."

His fingers skimmed over the wool, and shortly a scorching ball of orange ignited outside the cell. It spun and snarled as it grew bigger and bigger, spewing a fierce breeze that flapped my mouth and lanced my eyes as spears of hot coal.

I stooped to stay vertical, but even so my feet inched up in the air.

Soon the snarls fused with strident human voices and ZAP! The ball sucked me into its core, and a blink later spat me on the landing up a short flight of steps. I whimpered from the hard drop, a deadness overcoming my limbs.

Around me, everything was familiar, painfully so: the store where I forgot my basket, the lamppost with the maple leaf scar. Each prop in my supreme blunder set within eyeshot.

Egg white missiles, dozens of them, lingered overhead as pale kites frozen in an amber sky. I could see miles into the horizon. Where'd the haze go? I flopped onto my tummy, my pulse racing at light speed, and drank in the absurd landscape before me.

A spellbound audience wearing their Friday best pointed at the missiles and nattered, while a few yards behind them, Kubba and Councilor Ikhlaq beamed from the cleared blast site. That a canopy of explosives able to split their very atoms hung overhead drew no creases on their countenance. As usual, they were too busy rubbernecking to appreciate the apocalypse.

Rightward of the two, Muji lazed in an oversized mahogany armchair carved as a green-and-copper peacock, twirling his miswak stick, a wry smile stuck to his lips. While he wore the same salwar kameez, he wasn't the scrawny kid I remembered: now at least a foot taller and barrel-chested as a *pehalwan*—a traditional wrestler.

And on either side of the street, the shops sparkled with fresh coats of whitewash, and on their signboards glued posters impressed with the demon's smiling face. Bonga and his lackeys positioned behind Muji, their fingers resting on the handguards of snub-nosed rifles, their eyes steady but squinched in alertness.

Then I sighted him, and my blood boiled. Afi sat at Muji's feet, who was lovingly stroking his hair and kneading his shoulders. And though he moped, the gorilla didn't protest the treatment, and that alone convinced me he'd switched sides.

I long suspected Afi owned the spine of a sardine, but this barefaced evidence of my opinion wasn't comforting. Could I alone complete the mission? Then my gaze roamed to the streetlight beside them, and I gasped.

Chacha tied to its concave pole a foot or two above ground, his chin drooping to his breast, the horn missing from round his collar. If Muji had defeated his brother, this was the end. Should I surrender and beg for his mercy? I clenched my jaw, and yet my teeth chattered.

Kubba now stepped toward the crowd, demanding their attention. "Friends, we have foiled the enemy's dastardly plan to destroy Naya Chooran. To celebrate, we will turn this street into a national monument."

In response, they roared and sang Muji's name. Grinning, Kubba gestured to Ikhlaq, who half-bowed to the demon before striding forward.

"We're very fortunate we had a hero in our midst," said Ikhlaq. Then he made a sour face when pointing to Chacha. "Thank Allah he thwarted the vile creature who called in the bombs."

The crowd broke into furious booing, and they hurled eggs at Chacha and spat at him. But the geezer didn't stir, even as yolk streaked his beard, and eggshell shards clung to his now-floppy turban and dirt-smeared waistcoat.

"We're going to make the young man councilor," Ikhlaq continued. "Since this is a democracy, ahem, anyone who disagrees step forward now or keep shut."

His words struck me as a lightning bolt. Allah's wrath. If Muji became our leader without contest, the supernatural beings keeping this land won't intervene, and my suffering over days past was wholly for naught.

I stole below the steps and slunk through the buzzing clot of spectators. "No, he's not a citizen. You can't make him councilor," I barked, breaking through their ranks, my arms wildly flailing.

Muji's face darkened on a dime while Ikhlaq and Kubba gaped at me, thunderstruck. "How? How did you escape the dungeon?" the midget asked.

Bonga and company started toward me, their weapons leveled, their faces bleak.

I swallowed hard when facing the throng. "Your so-called hero is Majuj, the demon of old," I screeched. "He didn't save you, he's here to kill us all."

The crowd murmured among themselves, eyeing me askance. Then I pushed forward from a heavy shove and plunged to the asphalt.

"You're dead, kid," said Kubba, snarling above me.

"Listen to Kalia," Afi's voice exclaimed in the distance.

Then the midget fell back and Muji appeared, his features severe as a sheer cliff. The nib of his stick propped against my nose and he pressed deep into skin.

"This is how you thank me?" he asked dangerously. "Yajuj was right. I've become too mellow."

I coiled away from him, breathing short and hard, and leaped into a sprint. But ten paces later, a searing pain blitzed my limbs, as if an army's worth of bayonets were skewering my flesh.

On the verge of blacking out, I dove headlong toward the blacktop; the impact rendering me breathless and my beak bloody.

I willed myself to crawl, but it was no use. My arms and legs heaped beside me on the gravel, cleaved off clean as unused doll parts. They twitched and trembled, and though I sensed no pain, I shrieked and shrieked.

Soon after, my crown stung as I was picked up by my curls. When he swung me round, Muji's wolfish incisors were slavering, and his peepers bloomed crimson and feverishly whirled as a propeller. Then he was dragging me over the gravel, the bloodless stumps at my knees and elbows bruising and burning.

"I'm sorry," I wailed over and over to his deaf ears.

Chacha still dangled from the streetlight, lifeless, though for a twinkle I could've sworn his gaze was following me. Was he alive? Or had my pain brought on phantasms?

"A-are you going to kill me?" I asked, hysterical.

Muji laughed aloud in a chorus of voices both spooky and evil. "That's no fun, friend. I'm bored."

Chapter Six

Tickled to Death

We each have days we wished we were dead, but Allah's wrath, I'd never lived through this many together.

In Naya Chooran, my fellow wretches preferred death by rat poison or toxic moonshine, which naturally kept the town's occupancy rate in check. So, whenever I noticed someone sleeping on a sidewalk, I trusted they were the sadly departed.

But because mother despite her misanthropy always told me to value life, I'd toe their flanks to confirm such before whispering a brief prayer. They had nothing on them to steal, and so I never tried.

Since Allah frowned upon suicide, Councilor Ikhlaq dismissed the deceased as spineless ne'er-do-wells and everyone blindly believed him. Near daily propaganda on TV had them convinced their penury resulted from laziness, thus neatly covering up the fact our leader was the biggest dunce known to man.

Given the popularity of killing oneself round town, I bet many prospects should leap at the chance to giggle their way to the underworld. Idiots. I'd only wish dying from laughter on my worst enemies. Getting knifed in a shady back-alley was miles better, trust me. For starters, you weren't the punchline.

Muji had dragged my limbless figure over to his ornate chair and plonked me in the seat. There he twice patted my cheeks, smirking, ignoring my repeated pleas for mercy. Then he spun round and eagerly gestured to Kubba and Bonga.

They nodded, and straightaway jumped into action, shepherding the electric crowd into neat columns near me. My impending execution must've thrilled them, but in my drained state I cared little. It was a mighty struggle just to bottle my pain without retching.

Rightward and up the lane, excitement was brewing over a troupe of lank-haired musicians who'd showed up asudden in bright sequined vests and shiny curled-toe sandals. Each carried a short-sword belted at the hip and held a pair of silvery tongs the length of parasols.

Muji ambled to them and started an animated monologue I couldn't decipher, but to which they kept silent, their eyes fixed on him, their hands obediently tied at the waist.

Soon Afi split the columned people and joined the demon in a side hug, unresisting, the camouflage paint on his cheeks thin, maybe from rubbing against Muji's chest. Though he'd earlier piped up in my defense, now he avoided meeting my stare altogether.

The musicians burst into a raucous metallic rhythm, belting folk songs while their necks whirled as dervishes. Muji was flourishing his miswak stick and tapping his feet to the beat, the gorilla clumsily following his lead. The crowd too broke into claps and wolf-whistled their appreciation.

Shortly the demon parted from Afi and returned to me, reaching into his slit side pocket to produce a long, speckled feather which he raised toward his fans. "We're going to have some fun," he thundered to their loud cheers.

Muji stooped, touching the feather's tip to my knee stump. Then he was tickling me, his face brimming with mischief while the plume swished from one leg to the other and moved up to my elbows.

At once I was bucking and writhing, roaring with forced laughter, a torrent of tears wetting my neck. "Please stop," I said, my heart ready to rupture from the adrenaline.

Muji only cackled and tickled me more. "I'm having too much fun," he said, a bughouse grin twisting his features.

And then it got worse, far worse. He turned to the crowd, again holding up the feather. "Who's next?"

Before long, under Bonga and Kubba's supervision, the throng was queueing up to tickle me and chortle at my misfortune. Muji had retired to within spitting distance, squealing with glee and urging on the fiends.

Afi came to his side, sheepish, never looking my way. Hah, he kept acting macho and then abandoned me at first chance. Had Chacha's fate persuaded him we lost the fight? Not that I blamed him, given the prime villain's true nature, but without his help I'd never steal Muji's stick. Ah, was I to perish here?

Ikhlaq, I could tell, was toadying after Muji. He hung round the demon's heels, smiling at his advances toward Afi. The father's approval of their union was scandalous but unavoidable. Argh, this time I'd landed myself in a casserole of catastrophes. Even though I'd prided myself as too clever to fall for lamebrained schemes, the geezer had proved me wrong, damnably wrong.

With each new tickle, my very soul pinched and pounded, taut and ready to rend. Now and again I snuck peeks at Chacha, hoping he'd miraculously stir and rescue me, but the old-timer still tied to the lamppost, motionless. In my dark state, I beseeched Allah to grant him direct passage to the harshest tar pits of hell.

We'd failed. Someday these fools, or whoever survived the ruin, should call us martyrs, but today I'd die a traitor, from merriment of every shameful thing. How unseemly, how unmanly.

"Confess your crimes," Muji said when my crowing amplified to shrieks. "Confess now and your misery stops."

"I confess, I confess," I screamed for the millionth time, but again he feigned deafness. The godforsaken sadist only wished to prolong his amusement. I swung in and out of consciousness, my pulse petering into fitful spasms.

Then Muji and the mob tired of torturing me and gathered round the musicians. They broke out crates of sweetmeat which passed through their grabby hands, their chants of "Muji zindabad" punching through the spirited music.

My stiff shoulders sagged, and I drew swift but shallow breaths, my nape perching against the chair's back. Skyward, the hellish canopy of missiles still hung in the sky, unmoving. Oh, how I wished they'd lose their tether and scorch me to ashes already.

I awaited the end; awaited my sorry life to flash before my eyes and for blessed darkness to deliver me.

Yet each time I blinked, a glimmering marquee, the kind you find outside cinemas, loomed in my mind's eye. And blink by blink, the sign inched into focus until I could read its boldfaced text.

Wiggle, it said.

I grunted under my breath. Wiggle what, goddammit?

A creeping sensation traveled through me, the sense of my nerves tearing and repairing. I squirmed upright, biting on my bottom lip to snap out of the illusion.

Then appeared fiery grains of sand, familiar, akin to the giant fist from my dream. They took shape at the stumps of my knees and elbows, there spinning spiderwebs in glowing golden strands. And steadily, with the languor of water slithering toward a sinkhole, my limbs regrew.

An ecstatic whoop shot to my lips, but I daren't sound it. I could flex my fingers and wriggle my toes! Yet Bonga's lackeys, whose flinty stares fixed on me from behind the throng, did not react. And my severed appendages still lay on the street within eyeshot. Who did this? Were my new limbs a cruel mirage?

My thoughts cracked from a stir-frying sound, which cut into a storm of sweeping tones as though someone were tuning a primitive radio. I cringed, tossing round in the armchair, but the paramilitaries were unaffected. Was my mind tricking me?

"One-two-three, testing," a voice sizzed in my ear, before his unhuman laugh rattled my insides and drew a muffled yelp.

"We should get to the saving business, eh?" Chacha said.

Telepathy? I peeked at the lamppost, my heart thumping fiercely. For an instant his chin lifted off his chest and tipped sideways toward me, before retiring to its original state.

Bonga's men kept their icy glares but didn't move. Praise the Lord, my luck had changed. "I never thought I'd be happy to see you alive."

"Good, good," Chacha said, chuckling. "Now free me so we can dispose of my brother. There's not much time left."

Ah, the limbs must be his mojo. "Free you? Why can't you do it yourself?"

"Um, my horn vanished and this rope won't budge."

My pulse flatlined for a flicker and I groaned. "So, we're screwed."

"What? You're still Kalia?" he asked in a strained voice.

I hesitated. Wait, he couldn't see them? Then who remade my limbs? Were Zulkarnain's powers at last kindling in me? "You're one to talk, oh mister powerful demon," I spat. "Afi deserted me, Majuj almost killed me. What do you want?"

A long-drawn moan and nothing else. Chacha had reverted to catatonia, his wilted figure silently hugging the lamppost.

My gut bubbled from dread. Did he conk out for real? No, he sounded fine a second ago. Did I anger him then? Shit, shit. "You still there? I'm sorry, I'm sorry."

The guards had since joined Muji's party, which had shifted to the curb; shifted round large wooden tubs purling with a sticky-sweet red beverage popular with the locals. One after another, the revelers dunked their steel glasses inside and guzzled the rose-scented drink.

Meanwhile, the performers drew their swords and started a frenetic dance; their swishing blades and pattering feet twinning with the clattering tongs to give me a raging headache.

Kalia, you twit. If only you'd walked a different route that day, not been daydreaming, never involved yourself in this ceaseless nightmare. The only upside was nobody knew my limbs had regrown, in theory at least. But even if I stole away, for sure they'd shortly find me. And knowing mother, for a sheaf of cash she'd surrender me in a heartbeat. Ditto any of my glib siblings.

Chacha showed no signs of awakening. And his horn, I couldn't shake off its disappearance. The old codger wasn't senile enough to lose his precious artifact, so was he hiding it on purpose? Could I bluff my way out of this jam? I recalled him telling me Zulkarnain was a real smooth talker, but me, had I the skills to hoodwink an ancient demon?

"Mr. Majuj, your magnificence," I hollered to pierce the din. "I have something you want."

Muji cast me a sidelong glance, unperturbed, sipping on his drink.

"The horn, sirkar. Yajuj's horn."

Shock right away whelmed him, the whites of his eyes bulging, and his arm made a slashing gesture. The music and chatter dipped to a pin drop when he muscled through the throng, his countenance intense, unsmiling.

"What did you say?" asked Muji, puffing quick breaths.

I pushed back on the seat, gulping. Ah, he didn't see my limbs either. "His horn, you want it, don't you?"

He leaned over to lift me by the lapels, his crimson peepers whirling violently. "If you're lying, I'll hex you into a toad and squish you underfoot."

I heavily shook my head, simpering. "No, no. I swear I know."

Muji let me drop with a thud that banged my backside. While I grimaced, he strode over to his brother and studied him: his stick poking the geezer's ribs, his neck curving behind the lamppost to check the rope's bind.

"You're lying," he said, throwing me the death stare. "Yajuj wouldn't trust me with his treasure, much less you, a human."

As I suspected. Chacha was up to something, but what? I looked Muji in the eye, defiant. "Why the hell would I risk my life without insurance? I'm poor, not stupid."

Afi, Kubba, and Ikhlaq parted the crowd abuzz with curiosity and wore the same expression. The gorilla secretly winked at me, hinting things were going to plan, but I'd long struck him from mine. I had no use for fair-weather allies.

The demon stormed back to me, seething. "Tell me where and I'll pardon you. I can't keep him down forever."

His words gave me strength. Chacha wasn't dead, just biding his time to strike. I should continue the act until an opening presented itself.

Kubba padded up to Muji's side. "Now, now, councilor. This kid is a serial schemer. We shouldn't trust him, not for a second."

The demon was scratching his cheek while staring into space, his lips pressed tight. "Hmm."

I nervously shifted in the chair. Uh-oh, the midget was talking too much sense. At this rate, he'd convince Muji to disregard me. "How's this for proof?"

I vaulted to my unseen feet, started hopping round, and did cartwheels.

As one, the mob caught its breath. Two aunties swooned and fell into the arms of their equally freaked out neighbors. Afi and Ikhlaq screamed while Kubba stumbled backward, again and again saying, "impossible." To them, I must've appeared a floating hunk of meat with a talking head.

Muji was goggling at me, his wobbly stick trained in my direction. "H-how did you do that? Are you the warlock Samiri?"

An ugly purple-and-gold guppy conjured in my mind. I ceased my acrobatics and shrugged. "I asked your brother for guarantees. Anyway, there's no reason for me to oppose you anymore."

My pronouncement made him hoot with joy and pump his fist. "Hand over the horn and I'll reward you. Riches? Food? Toys?"

Kubba interrupted by insistently tapping the demon's arm. "No, no, councilor. That's a terrible idea."

Muji held up his palm to silence the midget. "How about candy bars, huh? A lifetime's worth?"

My brows bunched together. Why was he suddenly prattling as a toddler? "You cannot destroy Naya Chooran, got it?"

The crowd together gulped air and fearfully eyed their savior, who wore a hurt expression.

"What's wrong with you?" Muji said in a sobby voice. "Why would I wreck my kingdom?"

My contempt found speech as a loud snort. A real sneak, as Chacha said. By now the councilor and Afi had taken refuge behind the musicians, whose upraised swords shivered, their visages twisted from terror.

"Let him go," I said, pointing to the gorilla. "He's not your plaything." Then I looked to my severed limbs lying on the asphalt. "And reattach my arms and legs."

"But he's my favorite friend," said Muji, his fingers crooked as claws and quaking in anguish. "And I don't know how to restore your limbs. How are you even walking round?"

A tired sigh escaped me. Why'd the demon revert to a childlike state? How did he terrorize entire civilizations with such feeble will? I wrapped one invisible arm over the other. "Sorry, no deal then."

Muji pouted at first, yet soon he snapped his fingers, his sweet eyes-set-to-slits grin reappearing. "Why don't you borrow my treasure and try yourself?"

Oh, he folded? Wary, I plucked from his grasp the knotty flaxen twig, and rubbed its furry surface between my thumb and forefinger. Was he just distracting me? Was this a trap?

No magical energy surged in me from clutching his stick, though my forehead dampened from their pooled stares. If I snapped it in two, ought my life return to normal? Should I try?

There was an ear-splitting crash before heavy tremors seized the street. The next thing I knew, a lightning bolt struck the blacktop a stone's throw away, thrusting me backward with Muji's chair as my companion, his stick slipping from my clasp.

The sky had blackened and thunder rolled hard and true, as though the Archangel Israfil were prepping the final trumpet. And overhead, the missiles were marshmallows swaying in a sea of hot chocolate.

My lips were twitching without pause. Was this Chacha's doing? Must he grandstand to this degree? The mad old coot, he'd slay me too if he wasn't careful.

A crimson sandstorm had started in the street, whistling ominously, dulling the crowd's hysterical shrieks and wails. They sank to the ground, covering their faces, attempting to slink away from Armageddon.

Everyone except Muji. He stood frozen in his spot, peering wild-eyed into the storm.

A silhouette made visible in the tempest; humanlike, but enhaloed with blazing neon lights, the blistering squall its spectral overcoat.

"Damn," the demon said aloud, his palm slapping his forehead. "How could I forget?"

TAK-TAKA-TAK-TAKA-TAK. AHA-AHA!

Thumping dhol beats and Punjabi hollers drilled through the whistling.

On their own, the webs of fiery sand forming my limbs glowed angrier, and my curls stood on end as a feral cat's.

Then I heard it anew, the bestial laugh I knew well, and yet it curdled my blood.

— Chapter Seven —

Meet Mr. Walrus

The crimson sandstorm fell away stunningly; its grains dispersing as iron fillings that slacked to formless powder once the magnet distanced. The funereal sky too ceased its *Sturm und Drang*; shafts of light first pricking and then stabbing through the clouds.

From up the avenue, Chacha Kakakhel strutted toward us; his boom box slung over his chest and pulsing neon lights while pumping that god-awful tune. His polka-dotted waistcoat no longer flecked with dirt and his turban's crest had refound its perkiness.

I drew out a relieved breath and raised off the gravel on my forearms. While I thrilled at seeing Chacha in one piece, my gut needled from a growing unease and my goose pimples refused to retreat. Was I just nervy from his dramatic entrance?

Behind me, not a soul had stirred since the dust settled, though it was hard to tell from how they huddled together into an inchoate blob. The street was still intact, a miracle I thought given the supernatural fireworks from moments earlier, and on the horizon the missiles loafed in their precise spot. A wry chuckle squeezed my lungs. You'd think the geezer tossed jokey smoke bombs to scare us to death.

Chacha's boom box silenced as he neared, stretching his arms wide and arching his back, yawning. "Ah, I needed that nap."

Muji sounded a cry and dashed in my direction. He snatched his miswak stick from near the chair's overturned legs and aimed it at Chacha; his hands atremble, his pale face contorted with fury.

The geezer's stare fixed on me. "Good job, kid. I knew you could do it," he said, grinning. Then his mouth formed an O. "You can levitate? Is that your ability? Hey, Zulkarnain—"

"What're you planning, Yajuj?" asked Muji in a hoarse voice.

A wan smile broke over my lips. Hah, I'd worried for nothing. Chacha was still the crackpot I remembered. Thank heavens I'd bought us enough time, and now we'd defeat Muji and save the day. Hmm, for my well-deserved reward, I'd ask Ikhlaq for a house in the hills with modern plumbing.

I got to my feet and started toward Chacha, but straightaway Muji held out an arm.

"You're making a big mistake," he said, his stony gaze locked on his brother.

Chacha unslung his boom box and tossed it over his shoulder, but if it met the blacktop, there was no clatter. Then he made a sad face and shook his head. "Ignore him. He always was a sore loser. Let's finish—"

"He's been playing you," Muji shouted. "You don't know him at all."

My feet glued to the road, the goose pimples along my arm still taut. "So, we make you councilor and it ends?"

Chacha patted over his beard, peering at me with a bemused expression. "Ends, eh? That's the right word, I guess."

Muji fired off a furious grunt and swished his twig anew. A wink later, a vast shadow loomed over us, and when I glimpsed skyward my blood froze.

A pointy rust-red rock the size of a dump truck that dwarfed the missiles. Its tip twinkled crimson when it rocked back and forth in sync with the swishing stick.

"You can't do this, Yajuj," he said, crouching and planting his feet wide in a battle stance. "Give me your word."

Chacha kept stoic at the formidable sight. "You know my answer. I'm a man. I must do this."

Confusion at warp speed muddled my thoughts. Hey, who was the villain here? My arm outstretched toward Muji. "Stop! You'll kill us all if that drops."

He responded with an icy stare. "You idiot. You don't realize what you've done."

"He's Zulkarnain," said Chacha, tsk-tsking. "That was your first slipup."

Muji shot me a disbelieving look and kept it for his brother. "Have you completely gone insane? Forgotten everything we endured?"

The rock sank a few inches and tipped toward the lane, droning as an electric generator on overdrive.

Chacha offered a lengthy sigh. Then he stepped forward, his hands outspread before him. "Come on, Majuj. Why must you make this so difficult?"

Earlier I'd cowered on instinct, yet now I straightened and squared my shoulders. "Can someone tell me what the hell's happening here?" I said, my gaze flitting between the brothers.

"The missiles. He's going to destroy Naya Chooran," said Muji, his features stark. "I thought he'd changed after all this time, but I was mistaken."

Shock as a wrecking ball smashed into my solar plexus. "You mean…"

"Yes. My brother always was the mastermind."

My ears again rang with Chacha's insane cackle. "Don't worry, son, you and me are solid," he said, flashing me the okay sign. "And what do you care? What's Naya Chooran ever done but demean you?"

A thousand reasons streamed through my mind, none of which mattered. But as a man, I'd promised to defend this stupid town. "Why did you lie to me?"

Chacha faked surprise. "Oh, haven't you heard? One must keep one's enemies closer than friends." Then his corn-yellow teeth bared. "You're disappointing as Zulkarnain's heir, but that's helped me, so don't feel too bad, okay?"

"Enough!" Muji roared. "I won't let you destroy my kingdom." The drone grew deafening, the rock pulsating with greater and greater tension. "You've forced my hand, Yajuj."

Chacha's face crinkled in panic, and then he was backstepping, his palms facing outward and held to his ribs. "No, no, don't do this, brother," he said, whimpering.

My eyes tightened to a squint. Why'd the geezer's bravado crumble with such speed? Did he just enjoy senseless melodrama?

Muji didn't care for theatrics either, his fingers purposely flexing round the stick, his wrist bending toward the road. In that instant the droning turned to jet-plane shrieks, and the rock dropped a few feet with loud thumps.

I raced to behind the toppled chair and covered my skull, parroting the Shahada, casks of arctic water splashing over me.

No, no, I was a hero. I couldn't find my end as particles of flesh swimming in sewage, my essence befouled by stale urine and smelly cow pies. Unacceptable.

Chacha's anguished pleas for mercy reached my ears, as did Muji's angry dismissals.

My eyes shut tight as over and over I prayed. Allah, Zulkarnain, immortal beings, anyone. For the love of everything holy, please help me.

A tiny voice opened in my head: echoey, someone babbling deep in a well. For a few seconds, it rippled without form before saying, "Fine."

Chacha and Muji's voices had crescendoed into a shouting match before settling into an eerie lull.

A beat later, Muji bellowed and then a blistering shockwave tore through the lane, hoicking me as if I were a stray leaf and smashing me backward against a concrete pillar. Soon a kaleidoscope of colors splattered before my eyes; my vision akin to a crushed LCD screen.

Wincing, I massaged my neck and felt my sore kidneys. Another claylike blanket of dust set before me, and the stench of charred flesh was overpowering.

Should I sadden or celebrate? What was right? What was wrong? Was I now a sinner equal to the demons? But whose destiny was this? I was a savior, not an associate to slaughter. No?

Footsteps drew near, light but nimble. Chacha's mug stuck through the fog, and his sallow lips parted in surprise. Sans his shades, the swirling black hole atop his nose threatened to swallow my soul.

"Oh, you're unaffected by my counter spell?" he said, scratching his temple with the horn. "Guess I misjudged you."

Then his arm swept in a slicing motion and the dust round me melted as butter.

Muji stared at me unblinking, his face banged up and bloated, the side of his head stuck flat against the pavement. His body lay spread-eagled on his tummy, and jagged scorch marks ran to the small of his back.

I paddled backward on my palms, noisily hiccupping air, my heart lodged in my throat. Did I trust the wrong brother? Allah save me.

Muji's foaming mouth opened to speak, but he only gurgled. In the distance, Afi, Kubba, Ikhlaq, Bonga, the spectators, everyone, pressed into the pavement in similar fashion, quieted. It appeared an irresistible gravity pulled them to the earth's core and sapped their will to live.

Chacha dropped to his haunches and prodded my legs with the horn's mouthpiece. "They're invisible, eh? That's new."

My feet kicked the asphalt to propel me away from him. "Why are you doing this?"

"If you had the power to banish evil, wouldn't you?" he asked, frowning.

Allah's wrath. The geezer had absolutely unmoored from reality. "Yes, but…"

Chacha's hand waved round the street. "How's your town any better than Sodom and Gomorrah? I've razed half the planet for less."

No impassioned comeback arose in me, not a one. Maybe, deep inside, I believed he was right. "Everybody deserves another chance."

He grunted, eyeing the missiles. "They ran out of chances the moment they betrayed me. Well, I was at fault for marrying among peasants."

Then the founders of Naya Chooran…

"*Wakil*, is that you?" the small, echoey voice spoke anew. "Can you testify?"

And here I was, his mortal enemy reincarnated. Could he let me live? He'd nearly killed his own brother.

"I'm whoever you want me to be," I thought hard.

Chacha's fingers knotted together while he eyed me curiously. "Are you daydreaming, son? Last chance. You either join me, or well, you know."

"Is he the councilor?" the voice continued. "Are we needed?"

"Yes," I said aloud. "We need you now."

Chacha's head cocked to one side, and he grimaced. "Eh? What's gotten into you?"

I matched his stare. "This is about your sons, isn't it? Wiping out the town."

His oculus whirled fiercely. "This godless world needs me to purify itself."

Hah. Adults truly were weird. They convinced themselves they were doing the right thing, the honorable thing, yet never realized they were merely slaves to their particular experiences. What's worse, they believed these gave them strength, when in reality they were lifelong crutches.

Chacha uprose, his features steely. "What will it be? I can't dawdle all day."

The breeze was picking up, now bringing the faint notes of a music ensemble and the plods of marching feet. The geezer peered up the street, his brow furrowed.

A curious warmth coursed through me, tickling my brain. I sat up cross-legged. "I've finally figured out why Zulkarnain defeated you."

Chacha shot me the stink eye. "Didn't I tell you many times already? My sons," he said gruffly.

PA-PUH-PA-RA-CRASH-CRASH-PAH-PUH-PA-RAH.

The orchestra was swelling; a glorious cocktail of buoyant bagpipes, and clamorous brass, and clip-clopping snare drums. Before long, a lump of shadows came into view: uniformed, sporting peaked cap, shimmering as an oasis in the desert. "No, you're wrong," I said. "Zulkarnain's ability was one you could never possess."

"What? What're you blabbing about?" spat Chacha, twisting his horn into place over the black hole.

"Grace. You're a graceless man."

A whining sound; mechanical. The canopy of missiles moved, creaking, the shells drawing together into a giant bullet. Chacha inched toward the shadows, his fists doubled, muttering cusses. I snapped erect, bedazzled by their uniforms.

There were a dozen of them, the tall ones slotted back in the column. They strode nearer in lockstep wearing the colors of local wedding bands, their every nerve and muscle united in a sonorous melody.

Chunky belts with large silvery buckles cinched their overlarge scarlet shirts, while their two-toned slacks tucked inside alabaster-white galoshes. With each step their fringed epaulets fluttered, and on their sleeves stitched crescents in a golden thread.

"Who are you?" Chacha asked, his horn pulsing every color of the rainbow.

The diminutive bowlegged man heading the party, at first glance the geezer's age, raised his baton, and the band stopped playing. A bushy walrus mustache set under his panda eyes, and his breast packed with brilliant stripes and bars.

Chacha's leathery cheeks sheened with sweat. "Answer the question, dammit."

"Where's the wakil?" Mr. Walrus asked dryly. "The witness?"

Bloodlust infected the air, its serpentine tentacles arousing in me shudders. Once more the missiles creaked and Chacha slid forward, his countenance aflush with fury. "Don't ignore me," he said through clenched teeth.

I shot up my hand. "Me."

Mr. Walrus did a long double take, his posture stiffening. "Incredible. I would never have guessed."

"Is this your doing?" Chacha asked me, snarling.

A scrap of paper held up to the bandleader's nose, and he harrumphed, his throat booming as a foghorn. "Yajuj," he read. "For the crime of trespassing on and endangering this land, we must remove you."

"Fools, I'll turn everyone here to ashes," said Chacha with a sneer. "You have no clue who you're dealing with."

Mr. Walrus lowered the scrap and he suspired. "I thought you'd changed. Pity."

His form then flickered as an old TV; warping to a man berobed in green, his long beard snowy white, a domed prayer cap crowning his skull.

Chacha quailed at the sight. "Y-you. No, that cannot be," he said, backpedaling.

My incredulous stare darted between them. They knew each other? Were they the supernatural beings Chacha spoke of earlier? But why dress as wedding entertainment? "Please save us," I pleaded with Mr. Walrus.

My plea appeared to fuel Chacha's madness, for right away he cast off his cowardice and growled. "No matter.

I'd planned to avoid this fight by becoming councilor, but now I must turn you all to dirt."

Mr. Walrus was unmoved by the threat. "I see you're confused about your situation."

He gestured to his comrades, who at once set their instruments on the asphalt and began unbuttoning their shirts.

There was a resounding bang and then the whoosh of a welder's flame. The missiles were firing up one after the other, their tail engines as wakened dragons spewing fire.

Chacha wore the look of death when his clawed fingers raised to his chest, shivering, as though he clutched a soccer ball molded from magma. "And here I thought a man kept his word," he said to me, scowling.

I paid him no mind, my eyes nearly bursting out of their sockets. The ensemble's naked chests were kindling with starry spiral galaxies; a glittering tapestry of cyan and purple; and their peepers burned a fierce white.

The awesome view made Chacha hesitate, but then he took in a lungful, and his hands whipped downward. In a flash the missiles obeyed, plunging to the pavement, screaming.

I'd turned to stone, spellbound, watching them majestically rain on us. That instant I could've traded every shard of good fortune for a pair of wings, yet I couldn't imagine a better view before blowing to smithereens. The prospect of inevitable ruin held a strange allure.

My spell broke from a fleet of rubbery arms that shot into the sky as bamboo trees on steroids, and there weaved into a titanic fist headed for the missiles.

One by one, its fingers plucked the incoming rockets as though they were ripe mulberries. Then it rebounded toward earth, splitting into elastic arms which each held a missile, and returned to the musicians.

Forthwith they pressed the shells into their jammy chests, which started a series of violent explosions that for a twinkling shone them as a million suns.

Chacha sunk to his knees, hunched over, his horn fading to dull porcelain. "Preposterous. I came prepared. This is what I do."

Mr. Walrus's eyes ceased blooming. "As you destroy, we defend, Yajuj." His gaze turned to me. "Did you really have to free them?"

Chacha glimpsed me slack-jawed, and then he touched his forehead, giggling. "Oh, come on. Him? The kid's useless."

The garden. That door. Those coins bearing the runic symbols. A maelstrom of memories overcame me: visions of dust and sand, of cliffs and canyons, and plains of powdery funeral shrouds.

"Mr. Walrus," I said, clutching my head, cringing. "I'm the most qualified here to become councilor. You can ask around."

My advice, of course, was impossible. While the catatonic bodies spreading over the road stirred, they were in no position to dissent. In my estimation, they couldn't for hours yet.

The geezer gawked at me, though the bandleader's demeanor kept steady.

"Grace," I repeated to Chacha. "Zulkarnain bested you because you're graceless."

"How? Tell me," he cried.

"Can you imprison him too?" I asked Mr. Walrus.

He quietly nodded, and then his eyes gleamed anew, his hooklike fingers stretching toward Chacha. The geezer was waddling backward on his knees, blabbing of bribes and immortal life.

Soon there was an earsplitting swoosh, and the air round us sucked in as a vacuum cleaner. Chacha's torso was wet clay, by turn tearing and restoring, and with a chilling screech he disappeared inside Mr. Walrus's chest. Then the wedding band coolly buttoned up their shirts and stooped for their instruments.

My heart did a sprightly jig. Now I'd rule Naya Chooran justly. Find my mother a bigger house, make sure no poor went hungry at night. What else?

"How did you know I freed them?" I asked gaily.

This time Mr. Walrus's chin lifted to meet my stare. "We've done our part, Simoon. You must leave town or your attendant dust will render this land forever barren."

His band, their expressions severe, huddled round him, but he waved off their nerves. "The mighty djinn of the sirocco means us no harm. But to fabricate a family, false memories. Why go to such lengths?"

Inside me somewhere, a gear clicked and a bell tower rang in a new day. I studied my burly arms and blew out a long breath. "Many lifetimes spent burying humanity. I only wished to know why they so invoked God's wrath. Remember what made one a man. Was I wrong?"

"Well, I hate to admit, but Naya Chooran is no place for decent men," answered Mr. Walrus, bearing a lopsided grin.

"Why does it have to be so?" I protested. "Was I mistaken to foil Yajuj?"

He peered overlong at the immobile bodies strewn round the lane. "We each have our divine punishment, Simoon. Mine is to ensure the sinners make it to Armageddon."

My shawl formed of fiery sand now restored on my shoulder. "What about Samiri?"

"What about him?" he said, frowning. "He's a cretin. The worst kind."

A huge popping sound, as if a planetary soap bubble had burst. And thus dissolved the disquieting still that embraced Naya Chooran since the first missile fell, and in its place the *Adhan*—the call to prayers—sang through the city.

The lonely creature who uncountable moons ago sat under a dried olive tree smiled. "Hah, we men have it tough."

Come as You Are

The warlock Samiri again rode his spellbound rug to the summit of the solitary butte carved into a spear's tip. There he alighted and beheld the infinite sea of floury sand, his veiny fingers stroking his long wispy mustache flecked with gray, a satisfied smile curling his cruel lips.

Once, many kingdoms big and small bloomed along the banks of the two mighty rivers snaking to the world's end, but now their ruins entombed under Simoon's forbidding dust.

Allah's sense of humor amused Samiri. As with Shaitan, he'd seeded in the most ancient of djinns the absurd itch to rebel against his station, spurring the bleeding-heart Simoon to return to the realm of man.

Those demonic punks were small fry in the grand scheme of things, yet Simoon's obsession with righting a wrong above his pay grade was his undoing. But Samiri, unlike the djinn, saw into the future and thus he avoided futile crusades.

What age had the djinn entered? What misery had beset him? Either way, no news of him boded well for Samiri. His absence had proven a boon for the warlock, for it sped up his scheme to enslave the remaining human tribes.

Had he attempted such earlier, Simoon's hideous sirocco may have scorched him to ashes. The very notion of brawling with the brute made Samiri shudder. Admittedly, without the rune he long sought, he'd in a blink die a dog's death.

"Want candy?" a childlike voice said.

Samiri spun round to spot a boy perched atop a scraggy bump and holding out a tatty wicker basket. And though he smirked, his stare bore the cheer of a snowcapped lake.

The warlock's body tensed on instinct. Across these lands, what being beside him could climb to the hem of heaven? Was the boy, too, a sorcerer? "How did you get here?"

"How rude. A simple no would have sufficed," said Kalia, pouting.

Samiri's rug was flapping wildly, a flag helpless in a hurricane, and he took heed. Even in Simoon's presence, it'd never reacted so strongly. The boy was dangerous.

The warlock breathed deep, his palms raising to his chest and joining in the shape of a gun. "I will ask but once. Who are you? How did you find this place?"

Kalia's basket dropped into his lap, and he cackled. "Hah, I was such a fool. Yajuj and Majuj were evil, yes, but how did I ignore their ringleader who always whispered in my ear?"

Watchtower bells were blaring in Samiri's head while he speechlessly retreated toward the precipice. Inconceivable. How could this be?

A shawl made of flaming sand draped over Kalia's shoulder. "You're really something," he said, wagging his finger. "Keep your friends close and your enemies closer, huh?"

Samiri swallowed hard, sensing his reckoning was nigh. But whatever befell him, Simoon must die, and soon. He knew too much.

PART II

HOW DO YOU FREAKS FIND ME?

The Almighty Dollar

I can't imagine there's a soul alive closer to God than me. In fact, he; his cosmic jokiness, his infernal celestial majesty; takes such a keen interest in my life that he never tires of helping me ruin it. Hell, if I were an entrepreneur, I should impress on my forehead the phrase *divine pushover*, and charge people money to kick my backside.

And when the good Lord is not busy foiling my schemes to improve my station in life, he seeds in me the darndest ideas that unfailingly bring me pain. Is this the latest one in that ignominious line? The annoying little man inside my head believes so, for he snorts his displeasure anew, saying: Damn you, Holliday, nearly forty and still a fool.

Moments earlier, I crawled up the hairline-thin stairway of a seedy motel with busted lights to meet the kooky uncle they call Yaya. Presently he seats in a lotus pose on his beat-up bed and beckons me inside the boxy room. Though I'm careful, the wafer-thin door slams behind me, yet by a miraculous freak of fate it does not uproot and crash on my pate. But two steps into his room, the funk of cheap cigarettes flirts with weeks-old sweat to stagger me, and straightaway my eyes tear and my nostrils flare. Bah, for a famous seer, the geezer slums no better than a garden-variety hobo.

Unperturbed by my predicament, Yaya gestures with his thumb to the far corner of the room, to the spindly straight-back chair tucked under a desk that's missing a leg. I look askance at him, creeping past his bed and those obscene purple drapes, and drag the chair over a moth-eaten carpet with large fern tattoos.

Curses, his accommodations are a shrine to the colorblind, or those dead set on total blindness, and elevate the grandeur of my one-story hovel above the Hilton's. And now that I'm here, gambling blindfolded with Ipoh's loan sharks sounds more appealing, but courage is not one of my graces. Snoot and scorn? Well, that's another novel altogether.

I settle near him, but the moment my mouth opens to introduce myself, Yaya places a finger to his lips and shuts his eyes. Then he's chanting gibberish and swaying as if he's a wasted elephant; his dark inside-out jacket rustling under his tweedy newsboy cap. And every so often, he pauses his maddening ritual to check the hems of his two-layered pants that roll halfway up to his knees.

My shoulders hump as I draw my fingers through my sparse salt-and-pepper hair. Why, oh why, did I journey to this decrepit motel in the boondocks?

While he may be my last resort to turn round a lifetime of rotten luck, who knew this clown is thirty-one flavors of crazy? Argh, if only I could win the lottery, or the daily news raffle even.

Any effing thing everyone considers an achievement. Humph, call me human and don't you dare patronize me. I excel at that game.

I fussily wave my palm at him. "Hello? Can you help me? I don't have forever."

Yaya is chanting and swinging with greater vigor, as if he wishes me to self-combust from impatience. Right then, my twitchy nose surrenders to the toxic fumes floating round his room and expels an almighty sneeze. I yank out my plaid hankie, muttering cusses, and blow my beak so hard the lonely shaded lightbulb above his head rattles.

Yaya's eyes instantly wink open, and he bears a vacant smile. "That's a loaded question, son. Be more specific," he says, twisting the corkscrews of his bib-length beard.

My left arm throbs in time with my ticker. Specific? How specific can I be without laying bare my miserable existence? Can he read minds? Does he sense I don't wish to mourn yet another New Year's Eve?

"Should I keep buying lottery tickets?" I ask coolly.

His chin tucks into his chest when he snickers, his shoulders dancing. "Is that it?"

I eagerly lean toward him. "You mean, I should?"

At once Yaya crops up a cough and beats his chest with a loose fist, and then he draws an overlong breath to compose himself. "Sure, sure, you'll win. If you can help yourself, that is."

"Huh? How?"

"That's another loaded question," he declares with an impish grin.

I touch my forehead and suspire. This was a stupid, stupid mistake. Best to slink out the motel while my phone still holds a charge, and before the cops conduct their nightly raid. God knows what dreadful breed of criminals hobnob here after dinner.

"Alright, you're a lunatic. Goodbye," I say, rising.

That instant the door smashes open, and I jerk back into the chair. Three look-alike men; brawny, red-faced, and squat of nose; are struggling together through the doorway, thus attempting to debunk the laws of physics, and swearing at Yaya at the top of their lungs.

Yaya, though speechless, studies them sans a crease on his spacious forehead. My heart, meanwhile, is pounding with the ferocity of a runaway sledgehammer, my fingernails digging deeper into the seat's apron. Who are they? More pertinently, how in blazes did this geezer inspire such bloodlust?

After huffing and puffing for an eternity, the strangers realize their folly and storm inside in a single file.

Then the goon with the flaming nostrils aims an accusing finger at Yaya. "You killed our brother."

I glance over my shoulder, gulping down a yelp. There's the lone push-out window to my rear, but three floors are much too high for a Hail Mary leap. Curses, how do I escape this tinderbox?

Yaya shrugs at their accusation, busily picking his nose. "Well, it's not my fault the universe hates you."

His candor stuns them in their tracks, and they're gawking at him without a sound. Before long, their confusion swaps for rage, and raising a war cry, they lunge at him.

Argh, no choice. Why do I have a bottomless talent for finding trouble? I'm off in a flash to the window and wiggle its rusty cockspur handle.

The goon clutching Yaya's collar snarls at him. "Wise guy, huh? Why don't we toss you and your associate out the window? Then you can say hello from us to your beloved universe." He throws me a frosty stare that chills my blood.

Associate? Not a chance. "No, no, you're mistaken. I'm just here for a consultation," I say, facing them, my palms wagging to-and-fro.

The goon seizing Yaya's beard cackles. "Why? You want an early grave?"

Ba-dum-tss! My teeth gnash, and my fists curl into cannonballs. I'll laugh off the rich and powerful disrespecting me, but these rain slugs? No way in hell, no way.

I charge back to the chair and hurl it against the pock-marked wall with a mighty crack. They halt mid-assault to behold me dumbstruck while I hiss in the sinister tones of a feral cat. Next, my chest puffs out, and I shoot them my trademark death stare. "Let me conclude my business here, and you punks can parade him through town on a ballet dancing mule for all I care. Okay?"

The goon landscaping Yaya's beard, the only one sporting flecks of gray in his flattop hair, signals to the others, and forthwith they unhand the geezer and retreat from his bed.

Then he holds up his forefinger, glaring at me. "One hour," he says, and they lumber out the room grumbling.

My lungs briskly leak air while I double over, holding my gut that's knotted into a thousand twists. Ack, what was I thinking? That was mere inches from suicide by stupidity. Good thing I haven't aged gracefully, or they'd never have bought my act.

Yaya straightens his cap and pulls his jacket tighter round him.

Then he sighs, shaking his head. "I warned their brother not to pursue a harebrained business scheme, but did he listen? Nope. But off he goes, shooting himself from shame, and suddenly it's my fault."

I wearily prop the chair upright and plonk into it. Let's try this one more time, Holliday. There's no way I'm coming back, no way. "Can you be serious for a second?"

Yaya's head tips to one side, and he makes a sturgeon face. "The riches you seek always demand a great test, and personally, I don't think you're up to the task."

"Try me. I have nothing to lose," I say, holding his gaze with a steely expression.

"Alright, how much public humiliation can you take?"

A wistful grin breaks over my pallid lips. "I'm a career crossing guard. Public humiliation goes with the gig."

Yaya cants toward me, his knavish smile returning. "Aha, but can you sing amid a jeering crowd?"

My lips pucker on their own as I rapidly blink. Did he say sing? What's wrong with this fool? "Pity, I came to the wrong place," I say, again lifting off the chair.

Yaya bolts upright in bed, his hand reaching out in my direction. "Look, I can help you, but you must find a very special dollar bill. It should be a sword, but they're fresh out."

My fingers pinch my skinny hips while I glower at him. "I can't sing, can't sing worth a pot noodle. And who's they?"

He dismissively flicks his wrist. "No matter. Just pretend for an hour, play a dog if you must, and you're golden."

Sweat is misting on my cheeks. People laughing in your face, Holliday. Have you forgotten the last time? You peed your crinkly shorts and huddled in a corner to bawl your eyes out. Does your sorry life need more heartache?

Yaya chants and sways anew, soon producing a rinky-dink penlight from under his moldy pillow, which he flourishes with the spastic zeal of a gonzo orchestra conductor.

My frown intact, I'm pacing the floor, staring at the ferns. Another stupendous mess you got yourself into, Holliday. Outstanding job. The geezer is mad, madder than mad. Nothing good will come of this.

How long must you lay pipe to nowhere, huh? Shouldn't you accept things as they are, how they must be? That you're a scrawny black sheep in a family of prize-winning rams. Why wrestle with this reality every day?

I mop the sweat off my cheeks, groaning. "Fine, fine. What do I need to do?"

Yaya ceases his charade, and beaming at me, he playfully claps. "Perfect. First, you'll need a special summons."

Humph, where precisely does my tax money go? Do the fools in city hall need a five-year plan to repair a splintery park bench? This death trap hasn't seen better days in my lifetime, and then people say I'm a sourpuss without cause.

My palm skims over the bench's surface, and right on cue, a sharp sliver stabs my skin. I flap my hand, wincing, and suckle on the offended fingertip. Curses, so much for a thrilling afternoon hunt in the park.

Come at lunchtime and wait for directions, Yaya said. A summons fit for the superman of dollar bills; but does it glow when you touch? Or sprout wings? Or speak in ancient tongues?

No clue. Bah, that man puts the world's shiftiest politicians to shame. How long do I wait?

I warily lower myself into the only corner that doesn't yet resemble a medieval torture device and cross my legs.

Next, I check the scruffy linings of my neon work vest so they don't tangle in the woody veins and add to my debt. Then I rip open a pocket pack of sticky-sweet cookies and munch on them with the passion of a cow chewing cud.

The park sits between parallel lanes; an oblong patch of green topped with wild pointy grass that speckles with rusty steel rebars poking through jagged strips of concrete. A handful of high-spirited truants are playing soccer thereon, swerving round the rebars with the sharpness of cornered mice. I can't help but snort to myself. Ipoh, my hometown, is my mirror, a hot mess.

The blazing afternoon sun holds court bang in the center of the sky, and its attendants are two shy lumps of cotton-candy clouds, while over the thin, moist breeze sails the raw scent of wet earth. Other countries have seasons, I hear, but Malaysia only has summers ranging from hot to holy hell.

Should be thankful, though, for God often rains half the Pacific in compensation. Or does he mean to drown us? I won't deny many here deserve the punishment, besides me obviously. The big guy upstairs lolling in his heavenly throne owes me big-time for his untold gags at my expense.

I crumple the cookie pack and toss it behind the bench before slouching against its curvy backrest. One after another, long-billed birds flying together as shadowy triangles cross the horizon, and I blow a noisy breath. Ah, how I wish I could cast off my worries and join their exodus to a faraway land.

Twenty years a crossing guard. Twenty, for the love of God. Before long, the security agency will donate me a graveyard plot and a shovel branded with the company logo. Why, I need only ask and boss will gladly shove me into the grave and relay the dirt. Someone taps on my shoulder, insistent, each tap digging further into my blade.

My bleak thoughts disperse when I sight the teenage girl holding out a flier, and in the other hand clasping a capacious moss-green canvas bag stuffed with newspapers. She stares at me blankly in her standard-issue schoolgirl pinafore; an enormous mole peaking on her chin, her wispy hair tied back in a ponytail.

There's a peculiar stiffness to her posture, as though an ironing board sticks to her spine. I accept the flier, my eyes narrowing. "Why aren't you in school?"

"This is school," she mumbles, before wheeling round and ambling toward the winding lane behind the park.

I frown at her shrinking silhouette. Useless, useless parents. Why does the kid have to work? What're the idiots in government doing besides stuffing their bellies? I swear if they make me prime minister, I'll jail these do-nothing moms and dads my first day in office.

The yellowing flier snaps flat in my lap. So, what's the con today? I'm browsing through its contents when someone shouts in my ear, "You found it?" and for a flicker I jolt off the seat.

Yaya cranes his neck to study the flier, and soon he's hooting and spinning on his foot, resembling a deranged ballet dancer.

My palms ooze an icy sweat. Found what? No…he can't mean…"This isn't where I have to sing, right? In the afternoon? They'll mash me up into chowchow."

He stops prancing and squints at me. "This is your problem, son. You always give up before trying."

Has he lost his damn mind? Oh God, this could be another family reunion, or worse, the school play. They'll mock my onion nose and call me an ugly raccoon. My legs coil up on the seat and I pull a face. "Isn't there an easier way?"

Yaya slips off his sandal and pointedly smacks its cracked sole against the bench's leg, thus freeing up clots of dried mud which flop onto the grass. "Sure, you could always lie before rush-hour traffic."

I respond with a dirty look. What godforsaken summons is this? Okay, wait, keep calm. I could borrow a boom box from the guy next door who still has my frying pan, him with the annoying pooch. And binge on motivational videos to fortify me before the lynching. That'll make things easier, right? I scrub my chin, grimacing. "Can't do it, I just can't."

Yaya presents a stony face. "Son, Lady Luck herself gave you the flier, you of everyone in this city. Shouldn't you be more grateful?"

"That was her?" I ask, my breath hitching.

"She was today."

My lips purse as I stare yonder at the soccer ball spinning over the grass. This is most depressing. Lady Luck, the ancient hag, can shape-shift into a teenage girl, and here I'm adding wrinkles by the hour. Curses.

I spring off the bench and sweep the crimps off my vest. "Afternoon it is."

Yaya fakes a sniff, wiping at his nose. "You're leaving? I thought you'd buy me tea."

My head somberly shakes. "No, you fool, I must search for a prayer book, or three."

Heritage, my skinny posterior. I've never understood why Ipoh's biggest attraction is this sphincter of a cobbled path. How are columns of ho-hum shop-houses either side of the lane, graffitied with alleged art, worth the hassle? They may have tickled lovers in the tin mine days, sure, but now they're just a big fat nuisance.

Well, Holliday, this may be the last weekend afternoon your limbs stick to their original sockets, so savor them while you can. But that's easier said than acted out while I'm snaking through the needlessly thrilled masses in the needle-thin alley. And when the chubby boom box threatens to escape my grasp whenever someone's elbow spears into my kidney.

Around me, fussy aunties and bright-eyed tourists delight over pointless trinkets and shiny porcelain cats, which only heightens my urge to barf from the stink of street dogs breezing through the way. Focus, Holliday, focus. Eyes on the prize, lest you faint and make a doormat for these doofuses.

Seek the most crowded part of the street, the summons said. But how'll I survive an hour of egging, or worse, trained spitting? Bah, if I don't land the magic piece of plastic, that bearded half-wit will find a ticking time bomb in his mussy fuzz.

There, leftward, the recess between two smoky pillars, a somewhat safe place to park. I set the boom box away from the skinny gutter tracing the lane, a cantaloupe-thick lump swelling in my throat. Sorry, Phil Collins, your only sin is you crafted such memorable tunes.

I stoop to press play on the backing track, inhale a lungful, and then I'm bleating *Sussudio* at full volume. A clutch of passersby right away stop and stare, while others cover their ears and hasten away as quicksilver.

Others still, I'm guessing Collins's fans, shape their mouths into novel swears and offer me the middle finger.

Before I realize it, my voice finds an unflattering trill, and yet I keep braying as I must, now hoofing it to the chorus to appear sincere, if ruinously so. Never more have I yearned to be blind, to erase the unyielding scorn in their eyes, but I worry over the one egg that's well aimed at my crotch.

What's this? A beanpole of a man in baggy cargo pants with a massive gold chain round his collar is shuffling toward me. He halts within sniffing distance and his hands clasp at his chest in a beseeching pose.

My face flushes crimson. Great, another saucebox here to mock me. Why can't you let me be? I squat to silence the boom box, scowling at him. "What? I'll sing for as long as I want, you understand?"

"P-please," he says.

"Please what?" I ask, getting to my feet.

"P-please be careful."

A sinuous tattoo displays on his neck, a butterfly sampling nectar from a flower, and its sight sparks a sudden unrest in my legs. His stamp, I've seen it before in the papers, but why is the mob groveling before me?

Did the stress twist my features into a demonic toad's?

The man's face steels on a dime and he's stepping forward, reaching for his pocket.

I retreat on instinct, my arms shielding my chest, but right after my back butts against the rearward wall. Is he carrying a knife? Goddammit, no one here will jump in to save me from his kind. End of the road, Holliday. Your reward for trusting the geezer.

His fist is a blur when it meets my ribs, or so I sense before my eyes shut tight, but there's no blade ripping into my flesh. Instead, his palm slaps me backward and the next thing I see, a fistful of cash scatters in the air and rides a sudden puff of wind away from me.

Our eyes meet fleetingly and I'm struck by their sadness. Twice he pats on my arm, not saying a word, before spinning round and vanishing into the stream of passersby.

I don't dwell on his behavior since I'm busy examining the dollar bill stuck to my hand, which won't budge even when I waggle my wrist. Is it bewitched?

My breath is short and heavy as I peel it off to rub the glossy surface for secrets, yet there's no sudden light-show or angelic chorus to uplift my spirits. Grunting, I pull up my pants with overblown tugs. Bah, it's just a plain old dollar bill, but I should keep it on the off chance that it too is pranking me. The post-lunch crush of visitors thickens round me, as does the disquiet fermenting in my gut. Get back to work, Holliday, and leave before someone lances your lungs into Swiss cheese. I stuff the bill into my wallet and again crouch to the boom box. Now, what to violate next?

"Well done, bro." The mature man in a slick suit, his hands lodged in his pockets, wears an expensive smile.

Humph, isn't he too old to partake in the mockery? "Yeah?" I deadpan.

"Sure. You know who I am?" he asks, extending an arty embossed business card.

My jaw drops the second I scan the print. Huh, why is this TV big shot talking to me?

"Yes, yes, of course," I say, simpering.

"Drop by first thing tomorrow, will you?" he says, winking. "I think we can arrange something." Then he struts into the tide of strollers, who subliminally give him passage as their superior. An expansive grin lights up my lips, and I shimmy my shoulders, Bollywood-style.

The bill is the real thing! Must go launder my trusty old jacket posthaste, for his part of town is so posh they should knight it and demand visas on entry…

Argh, the old coot insisted I sing for no less than an hour. What to do? My torso tips against a pillar while I'm biting on my bottom lip, my toe absently tapping the boom box's seal-gray casing. Soon, the annoying voice in my head revives. Holliday, Holliday, we're special, can't you see? The magic bill's in our pocket, so why stay and risk an actual knife? Worst case, you'll apologize. You've always shone at that.

I nod seriously. Yes, that's a splendid plan. Truth be told, Yaya ought to commend my courage in the face of mortal danger. No sense trying to please others every day, right?

Ah, was there another morning this magical? Hmm, maybe once, back in third-grade when I gave a spirited speech on success before the class, which so impressed my teacher that she declared I'd doubtless be one. I've avoided her since I left school.

Stop it, Holliday, no depressing thoughts today. I rocket out of my squeaky wrought-iron bed and crank up the tiny portable radio on my rickety bedside table.

Then I dress up while prancing to *YMCA* in my spartan bedroom: delint jacket, check; crisp tie knot, check; spit-shine shoes, check. There's no stopping me now!

Holliday, Holliday, interrupts the irritating voice. Call a cab. If we pedal to the big shot's office on our museum piece of a bicycle, the outstanding people of poshville will release their hounds. Call a proper one though, not those red-and-yellow rip-offs stalking the bus terminal.

Fair point, I absolutely cannot be late today, and worst case, I'll dine on pot noodles tonight to stay in budget. Yes, this opportunity is worth the bellyache.

Thirty minutes later, I'm shading my eyes while looking up at the towering glassy skyscraper and whistling in awe. Here uptown, the double-wide roads sparkle as though they're virgins to crushed soda cans and retching drunks, and the marbled plazas shimmer as if someone unwrapped their gift box yesterday.

I frisk up the two dozen steps to the sleeky portico, soon passing a duo of grim cops who lead a handcuffed man past me. Wow, what did he do to deserve a black towel over his face? Oh well, not my problem. My grungy loafers squeak over the palatial lobby's polished hardwood as I needle through tight clusters of art deco seating to the wavy underlit front desk.

The chic woman behind the counter is busy making duck faces to a compact mirror.

My hands set on the smooth leaden countertop, and I harrumph. "Mr. Slick is expecting me."

She casually motions to the monolithic sliding doors. "They arrested him a few minutes ago."

A grand piano drops on my chest. "What? Why?" I ask, breathless.

"He conned many people, I hear."

I stagger aside from the counter, choking on a scream.

Was it him under the black towel? Goddammit, why me? The one time I catch a decent break and presto, it goes poof.

"What happened to the lottery?" Yaya is flanking me, scratching his nose, his brows bunched together.

I sink to my haunches. Curses, why's he here at the worst possible moment? Why is my life overflowing with them?

Yaya reaches under his newsboy cap to produce his penlight, which he then points dead into my peepers. "Did you follow my instructions to the letter, hmm?"

I wince, my palm raising to hide my eyes. "That infernal bill is still in my wallet. Didn't sing for long though, they were ready to skin me alive."

His foot angrily stamps on the hardwood. "Lady Luck does you a favor and yet you still fail? What's your problem?"

"W-what should I do?" I ask, whimpering, yanking my tie loose. Yaya's lips curl as he faces away. "Don't pity-party me, son. I know your kind well."

"Please, please give me another chance. I made a mistake. Got carried away by the attention."

"And why should I do that?"

"Because I'm tired of free-falling," I say with a wan smile.

Yaya's hawklike stare bores into my soul while he's drumming the penlight on his layered pants. Then his eyes roll upward, and he heavily sighs.

"You must regain her sympathy, I suppose," he says. "Though if I recall correctly, only one person ever managed the feat, and he was a far nobler creature than you."

I arise in a twinkle and inch toward him. "I'll do whatever you want, please."

"Six," Yaya says gravely.

"Eh?"

"As him…what was it now?…Susus…Theseus?" he absently tugs on his rustic wool scarf, "Anyway, six is the number of your redemption. Do you accept?"

The geezer's finally gone bonkers. "Uh, accept what?" I inquire, my forehead creasing.

"Your quest, what else?" Yaya retorts. "One labor for each week till year's end, though you won't know when or where. And each time you answer correctly, you'll land a clue leading to Lady Luck. Clear?"

Life ebbs away from my limbs. "That long?" I ask in a cracking voice.

Yaya chuckles, his finger wagging back and forth. "Ah son, you'd kill yourself if it didn't."

⌘

The Coffee Crusader

I'll never, ever understand this: how the hell does a city teeming with charlatans and ne'er-do-wells run low on its only saving grace? This is calamitously unfair. I have so few reasons to live, yet God insists on picking them off one by one. Why, why of everything unholy in Ipoh does the cosmic joker only make Chinpo coffee disappear? Curses.

My forehead is drumming the flimsy vinyl tabletop at metronomic interludes, a sob sticking halfway in my throat. A smattering of patrons, too cheerful for my blood, are snacking and chattering round the grotty open-air diner that reeks of grease and fried noodles. And around them, a jaded troupe of servers in red aprons dawdle over the stained eggshell tiles holding clipboards the length of pocketbooks, their pens tucked behind their ears.

I rest my head flat on the coarse tan tablecloth, soughing. Can I ask Lady Luck to award me a lifetime's store of Chinpo if I complete the quest? For me, riches hilled to the peak of

Everest are worthless if I can't swing out of bed. As for the quest itself, will I survive till the end?

Given the misery Yaya put me through to find the summons, he must've laid many monstrous traps for me to overcome. I creep upright on the severe steel chair, the empty glass beside my wrist clunking from my twofer digital watch.

Bah, there's no point cycling from diner to diner anymore. Is Chinpo's disappearance one of Yaya's tests? If so, the geezer was right. To compress the quest any shorter will doubtless kill me.

Sigh, since I'm here, I may as well stay hydrated and live to sulk another day. Remember those motivational tapes and their message, Holliday. Life, unless you won the birthday lottery, is a gut-wrenching, soul-sucking marathon. My hand wearily raises and I shape my lips to whistle, but in my languor blow a raspberry instead. Soon a slack-jawed server with a pencil mustache shuffles up to me.

My fingers form a steeple atop the table. "When will you have Chinpo again?" I ask grimly.

"Uh, don't know, boss. Still out of stock," he deadpans.

Isn't this nice? Nobody knows when the lifesaver will return, yet the morons multiply without restraint. My fist beats on the table as if it owes me money. "Then why are you in stock?"

The server blankly holds my stare, awaiting, I presume, for his brain to translate my simple question into Neanderthal grunts and squawks.

"Get me more lime water ASAP," I say, my fingers kneading the ridges of my brow to relieve the migraine firing through my skull. I needn't have bothered, for the tablecloth's loud flowery patterns are custom-made to deliver brain damage.

The maddening little guy inside my head groans. Holliday, Holliday, without Chinpo, it's a damn miracle we put our pants on right this morning, but miracles by definition don't last. Any more waiting, and we should start kidnapping old aunties. One of them buzzards must have a box of the magic powder stowed in her musty pantry.

I mumble in agreement, pinching open my eyelids to forestall the incoming swoon that any minute now will throw me headfirst to the ground, slavering. Should I head to a hospital clutching my heart? A shot or three of pure adrenaline should return my sobriety, for now. Hmm, do hospitals stock Chinpo?

"Long time, bro," a breezy voice says above me.

I flinch and nearly topple backward. Those beady peepers and that hook nose could convince the dead to change graveyards. Hooky, the crossing guard-turned-delivery boy, peels off his fingerless gloves and drops into the seat opposite me.

His puckered lips crook to one side. "Jumpy again, huh?"

I scrub my face over and over, wishing he's a daymare. Why does his kind always assume I'm itching for small talk? Maybe I need to scowl more. Or wear a hat that reads vamoose, or else. "Yea, I guess."

He titters while tugging at the maroon-and-cream polo shirt of his trade. "No kidding. Your face says you tripped to hell and back in a rickshaw."

I throw him the death stare. How, how do you freaks find me? "Having fun?" I ask in a serpentine hiss.

Hooky raises his palms in surrender, his face cast into a sheepish grin. "Sorry, sorry. What's wrong?"

My nose once more meets the tabletop, and I begin in a tone that flutters as toilet paper nailed to a jetliner:

"I need my Chinpo. They don't have it. Nobody, nobody has it. It's like the earth swallowed the whole damn company."

He slaps his thigh, chuckling. "Is that it?"

My stink eye returns and I puff a noisy breath. Sure, you join in too, why not? Let's all mock my suffering. Someday, sure as the sun rises, I swear I'll ban your brood on this planet.

Hooky's lips make an O, his palms waving in apology. "I mean, I know where you can find Chinpo."

I eye him askance. "Yea?"

He nods cheerily. "The members of my club love that brand. If anyone has a spoonful left in Ipoh, it's them."

My distrustful expression stays. Though I want his claim to bear true, not too long ago his insouciance sent me on a panicked hunt around town for my missing traffic lollipop. The idiot later confessed he'd borrowed it and forgot. Well, Holliday, what're your choices here?

I shift upright in my chair. "Where? Can I join?"

"Sure, what're friends for?" he says, winking. "I have errands to run, so why don't you go first? It starts in an hour. A special meeting, I hear."

Then Hooky glimpses round the diner in a conspiratorial fashion before flicking a plain round-edged card over the table. "Your pass."

I fasten the card between my fingers, my spirits lifting. The Coven, eh? Fishy name, but who cares? And a three-digit number. Okay, I'll smuggle out as much Chinpo as possible for later. No point fretting over etiquette in my condition.

"What do you guys do there?" I ask, nonchalant.

Hooky makes a lopsided smile. "Good times, bro. You'll fit in nicely."

For the love of God, serve the coffee before my inner mongrel arises and I'm snapping at your heels! I reach under my plastic mask with the long swirling mustache to claw at my chin. Why does this infernal thing constantly itch? Then, gritting my teeth, I clutch the thin black candle they passed out at the entrance tighter in my fist. Damn you, Hooky.

Around me seat row upon row of shadowy figures in hooded robes and masks, their murmurs rippling across the dark pillared hall as whispered hexes. A compact stage with sable carpeting sets before us, below a nest of half-lit spotlights screwed to the low ceiling. And a strange nutty scent hangs over the place; pleasant, but a tad oppressive for my sensitive schnoz.

I smoothen over the goose pimples on my arm and hunch in the curvy banquet chair. Curses, is this the grand gathering of trainee Satanists? Serves me right for trusting Hooky's notion of a good time. If these mooks are Chinpo loyalists, I must at once rethink my life choices.

Before I know it, a mighty yawn threatens to escape me, but right away I clench my jaw. Beware, Holliday, whatever accursed majesty called this meeting will have spies in the audience.

Then the sound of snoring carries to my ears. At first, it's someone behind me, and then someone a few seats removed. Hah, I'm being paranoid as usual. A quick nap can't hurt since these clowns are taking forever to start the meeting.

My neck perches against the backrest, and I close my eyes. "Wake me when they bring out the blessed nectar," I mutter to myself. Zzz. Zzz. Zzz.

TARAN-TARA, TARAN-TARA!

The hall sound setup explodes with trumpets, the

helter-skelter of which must match a twenty-one-gun salute on Judgment Day. I bolt upright, spooked, and straightaway my unsuspecting neighbors greet my elbows in the kisser.

The hooded legion rise as one, whooping with joy, pumping their candles in the air. I do as them, ignoring the pained cusses of my victims, my pulse racing. Are they finally bringing out the Chinpo? Please let it be so.

But it's a wizened old man in white robes carrying a wireless microphone who's scaling the stage at a two-toed sloth's pace. My neck bends forward, my jaw hanging loose at his sight. This is a horrible mistake. How could anyone get excited over him? His own mother couldn't.

Whitey outspreads his arms to signal the audience to seat themselves. Then he clears his throat and performs an endless mic check of *umms*, *ahhs*, and *one-two-three*.

I sink into my chair, scowling, and snuff out the candle in protest. Goddammit, where's a noose when you need one? For him, I'll happily play executioner without pay.

"Friends and countrymen. We tire of the corporate elites that fleece us year after year," Whitey says with the busy hand gestures of a sign language interpreter on TV. "No more, we say. It's time to reclaim our dignity."

The hoods roar their approval, to which he beams and responds with feeble fist-pumps. My eyes roll back into my head. Oh, Hooky, I hope you're bleeding dry in a ditch somewhere surrounded by wolfish rats. Argh, should I leave?

"Ahem," Whitey says, still grinning, his palms now gesturing rearward to the inky side of the stage. "Let's all welcome our savior, the man who made today possible."

BUMBADUM-CHICKA-CHICKA-BADABUM.

This time clamorous rock music rattles the hall, and in tandem the spotlights come alive and are whirling as dervishes, casting their multi-colored shafts onto the stage.

My neighbors again get to their feet and are swinging to the racket, while I cover my ears and cringe. May the good Lord smite these fiends. Wasn't my raging headache from caffeine withdrawal punishment enough?

A figure emerges from the black behind the stage; a dwarf sporting an eye-patch and a flamingo-pink suit who struts to the center and grabs the microphone from Whitey.

I rub my eyes and blink on repeat to make sure I'm not hallucinating. His arrival shouldn't surprise given the tasteless warm-up act, but this…he…he's the savior? Wow, did I step into an interstellar wormhole instead of a club meeting and arrive in idiot-land?

"Friends, congratulations," Pinky says in a booming voice. "At long last we've ruined Chinpo." The hoods erupt in mindless applause as he's prowling the stage, his arms victoriously raised in a V.

My hand presses on my twingeing gut. No way, no mother-loving way. I pop my ears with my palms again and again. Nah, I must've heard him wrong. By right, the most any club Hooky belongs to should scheme is cleanly cracking peanuts with their big toes.

"I'm offering you a fresh outlook, a reason to love your new jobs," Pinky continues. "Once we kick Chinpo out of town, I promise all of you'll get joining bonuses."

His fans are wolf-whistling and chanting his name while Pinky lowers the microphone to whisper to Whitey, who without delay scurries off-stage.

My chest tightens into a python squeeze. Who are these fools? Unhappy Chinpo employees? How dare they? I yank the robe's hood off my head and fussily paw my scalp. What should I do? Slip away and call the cops?

PARAP-PARA, PARAP-PARA!

The vile trumpets lance my ears anew when Whitey wheels onstage a clunky contraption the width of a microwave; gunmetal gray with pipes that angrily puff steam sticking out from its plated surface.

I swallow hard and my throat scratches as sandpaper. Curses, he wasn't fibbing. It's a bomb, or an evil robot. Either way, the dastardly midget plans to decimate Chinpo headquarters.

Pinky turns to the hushed crowd, gleefully rubbing his palms together. "Welcome to the future," he says, pointing to the contraption. "This miraculous coffee maker will rid us of Chinpo forever. And today, one of you fine folk will do the honors."

The masked swines are caroling his name in a singsong while the rim of my mouth upturns from confusion. Huh? How will that drive Chinpo into retirement? There's more to this scam, I bet. Argh, if only I'd upgraded my phone to one that takes decent video, because as things stand, it's my word against theirs.

The hoods in the next row are clapping in my direction, jabbing their fingers toward the stage. I react with a vacant stare. What's gotten into them?

"He called your seat number, man," someone yells over the commotion.

Oh? I instantly pull to my feet and meet Pinky's stare, who's beckoning me with brisk flaps of his wrist.

My sphincter tightens on reflex. Uh-oh, I'm not the virgin sacrifice today, right? Their crash test dummy to prove the machine works?

I slither through their robed legs in my trek toward Pinky, and the entire time they're cupping their hands round their mouths and shouting words of encouragement.

My tense face softens into a simper, and I acknowledge them with slight nods. This is nice. I could get used to this.

Five minutes; it takes hardly five-effing-minutes to revive my rotten luck. I'm clutching my kneecaps, begging them to cease shivering so I can flee.

Absolute chaos rules over the hall; robes are fluttering and swishing as a colony of bats, their owners hollering and wailing as they stampede toward the exit. Slashes of electric lightning sizzle round them, and the acrid stench of smoldering plastic steadily chokes the air.

Sweat is pooling as rainwater on my back and slinking into my undies to have me squirm. Bah, so much for the midget's miracle machine. Maybe the warlocks at Chinpo uncovered his intrigue and put a counter-hex on him.

Whitey is circling the stage with his robe on fire, shrieking. He breaks into wonky cartwheels; he furiously rolls on the floor; and he runs and runs. I don't wish this on my worst enemy.

My legs at last abide, and posthaste I pluck off my mask and robes to toss them aside. Though the smoke has set fire to my lungs, I summon the strength to toddle over to the stage lip. I can't die with these traitors, never. A high-pitched snarl cuts through the pandemonium to distract me.

Pinky, his face screwed up into a wrathful demon's, is rushing at me headlong, wielding as a spear a shiny thermos the height of a fire extinguisher.

Uh-oh. My bladder readies to leak when I spin round to take off, but right then the thermos slams into my ankles and floors me onto the carpet.

I flop onto my back, whimpering, my eyes stricken with terror, when Pinky scoops the shell and props it against his shoulder with a splash. In that moment, a sliver of sunshine touches my heart. Is that coffee? Chinpo, is that you?

Pinky growls beastlily, winding his hips to swing. "You effing idiot, the lever, not the switch. How many times need I tell you? You've ruined everything."

An unusual lightness is filling my limbs. The thermos, it must be a sign. Yes, my darling Chinpo recognizes my loyalty.

The missile-shaped container is pitching downward in slow motion, for I sense his every sinew flex and his every muscle strain.

Bah, give it your best shot, demon. I handily dodge the blow by vaulting backward into a crouch.

He grunts and follows up with a vicious side swipe, but before he can complete his swing, I release a swift kick to his knee.

Pinky briefly staggers from the hit, but soon after sounds a war cry and is barreling toward me; the thermos raised aloft his head as though it's a hatchet.

My breath shortens into frenzied huffs. Think, Holliday, think. You must disarm the pint-sized scourge before he pulps your mug into a chapati.

Metal thuds against the floor inches from my toes. Now! I lunge for his wrist and bite into bone for dear life.

Pinky throws his head back and squeals, his weapon slipping to the floor with a clang. Huzzah! While the midget is swatting his hand from pain, I snatch the thermos and slant it before my chest as a broadsword.

"My turn," I declare, sliding my foot forward to imitate a stoned samurai. Yes, I am the one and only coffee crusader.

But there's a swoosh, and the next instant I'm soaring sideways after Whitey dropkicks my kidneys. Ack, I completely forgot the cartwheeling geezer.

I crash into the carpet and start rocking to-and-fro, hugging myself in agony. Whitey clambers to his feet, brushing his flame-licked robe, and shoots me a thumbs-up while weakly smiling.

Then Pinky lurks into view, his face scrunched up from fury, and he punts my shoulder with his pointy shoes. Before long they scamper away and I roll onto my side, my temple throbbing, me reciting my entire corpus of swears.

An unpinned grenade for Hooky's birthday, a bouquet if I can track the right black marketer. I'll even hire a photographer to capture the blissful moment of him bursting into fleshy ribbons.

Polished steel. It glints within spitting distance, and my frayed nerves soothe. Only Chinpo can save this horrid day. I creak upright, lock the thermos underarm, and limp off the stage.

Bright sunlight gushes from where the hulking double-doors should be, and round the hall, a handful of figures in hard hats are spraying foam on the flaming wall sockets.

My arms reach out groping air as I cross the arena, knocking into toppled chairs, and nearly tripping over discarded masks and robes. The exit nears, and so my limbs find strength anew. Soon this nightmare will end.

Yet one step out the doorway, and I hastily retreat to spy from behind the wall.

The pea-gravel patio outside glimmers from a battery of police lights, where a half-dozen po-faced cops are grilling the hapless chumps who ran out in their robes.

My neck pulls back, and I squat against the wall, sulking. Argh, why now? Can't I ever catch a break? The thermos' tubular shell clinks from my tapping fingers. Hmm.

Carpe diem, Holliday. If this fails, you can always feign terminal sickness. In your state, you could convince any judge and jury of your impending demise.

The cops are busy stuffing the stragglers in their cars and gabbing on their radios. This is it. The thermos hides my face when I sneak outside and swerve in the opposite direction.

A foot, then five. I lick my parched lips. Not much further and I can zag behind the building.

Pitter-patter, a skip, and a canter. No yelling yet, or stamping feet. They didn't notice me? This is depressing, depressingly familiar.

I curve the corner and start into a furious sprint toward the lush shaded garden at the back, and then beyond its tiered stone fountain to where a pebbly trail shows itself. I scurry through the trail's prickly thickets and stumble into a suburban lane where the terraced houses are apple-red. Freedom!

I sink onto the sidewalk and my lips greedily meet the thermos tap. Chinpo, my beloved, how I missed thee. Thank you, thank you for delivering me from the evil midget.

What's that smell? Burned toast? I cease guzzling the liquid goodness to sniff the air. Nope, no houses aflame either.

"Hey, can you share?" a scratchy voice says. Pinky, his fancy suit now streaked with soot, totters out of the thickets.

I spring upright, gripping the thermos for a shield. Bah, useless cops, always letting the ringleader get away. "You. You have some nerve."

Pinky draws a white hand-towel from inside his coat and waves it at me. "Something to drink, please."

No bulges in his suit, no sharp edges, nothing that portends a hidden weapon. Should I rearrange his face for ruining my life? But he cuts such a pathetic figure.

Keeping my distance, I lob the thermos at him, thunderstruck when he's suckling on the tap as if it's mother's milk. "You drink Chinpo?"

Pinky's features pinch as a prune. "Who doesn't? I'm evil, not an idiot."

"Then why the hell are you trying to destroy the company?"

A police radio is crackling nearby, faint but incoming.

Pinky nervily glances toward the thickets. "A year's supply of Chinpo?"

"Oho, you're bribing me to save your skin?" I ask, chortling.

"Either that, or no coffee for months. They can't replenish—"

Pinky is clasping his throat, turning ashen, and he's chuffing and wheezing nonstop. The thermos leaves him and bangs against the asphalt while he punches his chest over and over, his eyes bulging from mortal fear.

Dread is pinging through my chest when I touch my neck for new lumps. Was it the coffee? Should I help him? Curses, will I share the same fate? Then Pinky doubles up, wildly coughing, and gobs out a thin projectile: a slimy piece of plastic.

I back away from him, glimpsing round for witnesses. Screw this, I should bail before the cops appear. Hmm, something's not right.

I drop to my haunches, to the plastic-coated paper the size and shape of a tea-coaster. Is that childlike sketch a cycloptic eye? And a signature at the bottom. *Y-a-y-a.* Huh?

A hankie swiftly produces from my pocket, and I flip the paper to sight two bold dots on a straight line. Is this a clue? Did I answer right? What was the question? Is there a question? Argh, must the geezer always act cryptic?

"Who are you?" asks the cop, glaring at me from the thickets.

Super, the cavalry is here. I snap erect and point to the sidewalk. "He's the one—"

A lonesome eye-patch rests on the curb and nothing else.

It takes everything I have to suppress a primal scream. The weasel must've slunk away with the coffee at first chance.

The cop folds his arms, his countenance mirroring a rocky cliff. "What are you doing?"

My heel is pawing the asphalt and a nervous giggle leaves my lips. "Trying to find Lady Luck. You see her round lately?"

⌘

— Week Two —

Part-Time Hero

Yep, this country needs a war. The dire lack of ceiling fans in Ipoh's open-air diners is unacceptable. And since they're fashioned from old copter blades that whirl with less urgency than the village drunks playing chess, we need more downed choppers.

For the millionth time in the past hour, my palm mops my clammy brow while I'm fanning myself with a crumpled newspaper. Curses, another nuclear evening. Too many in a row this week. My plate as yet hills with fried noodles, appetizing I'm told every time I grumble to the servers, but this grub I daren't doggie bag for a hobo.

Sigh, what wretched luck the only diner in walking distance of my place is the sewer of the hospitality trade. The minute actual money blunders my way and I can quit my lease, I'll torch this place as a public service.

The wall-mounted TV does little to lift my mood. Local news is busy fawning over a volunteer firefighter who they claim saved triplets from a downtown inferno. The gent, a photogenic twenty-something in black overalls, speaks in the solemn tones of a sultan on coronation day.

My elbow now sets on the kitschy tablecloth, my hand cupping my chin while I gaze deadpan at the screen. Bah, in this backwater, everything's news.

Mister firefighter now outthrusts his jaw, faking a serious expression. "Yes, we welcome recruits, but mind you, we have high standards. A firefighter is like Superman, you know? One minor mistake and many people die."

A sudden fever seizes my body, and I snort under my breath. Pish, every fleeting celebrity thinks he's Tom Cruise in Top Gun. Why's Lady Luck so smitten with them, huh? Curses, when is my turn to shine?

"Oh, go screw yourself," I unwittingly bleat, and right away a myriad of stony eyes stare daggers at me. I shrink in my seat, swallowing hard, timidly peeking at the diners.

A tap-tap in my brain and the little man clears his throat. Holliday, Holliday, if we meek ever inherit the earth, we should chuck our boss into the mythical lake of fire. The cunning weasel halved our work hours citing budget cuts, yet while we dine on this mockery of food, his purse fattens as his belly. He shows not an ounce of respect for our years of service, yet has the crust to offer us false hope. Don't forget what dad said, there's no such thing as temporary poverty.

True, true. My chin lowers to my chest and I suspire. How long before my meager savings impel me to staple newspapers for underwear? One test closer to winning Lady Luck's favor, I hope, but dots and lines? What do they mean? Another effing bridge to nowhere? Argh, where is that half-wit, Yaya?

A phone number pops up below the smug firefighter inviting volunteers to register, and I faintly smile. Well, I'm working half-days, so what's the harm? Given a hard hat and a swanky uniform, can I too become a hero?

The ghost-white wall behind the sturdy glass-top desk fills with framed pictures of the cocky brat from TV posing with a cast of local luminaries. My slack jaw resets when I lower myself into a ladder-back chair before the desk, curbing the urge to cuss enviously. Look at that smirk. A real hotshot, eh? Must be nice.

Good thing I booked an afternoon interview before heading to work. Hah, I'll surpass him in no time and become the toast of the town. Young people today don't realize the infinite potential of desperation, more so when you're knocking on middle age's door with a personal biography brimming with bummers.

Besides the pictures, his office is bare and soaking in the wet scent of industrial antiseptic; the former by design, I suspect, to direct people's attention to his wall of glory. A sloping console sits to one side of the desk, housing an array of phone handsets, while angled in the far corner is a whiteboard-on-wheels taped with colored strips.

The door behind me lashes open to let in three men sporting black jumpsuits whose heavy boots clack over the slick ceramic floor. Hotshot's two companions are shorter and rounder, and they stay at his heels with the reserve of houseboys. I instinctively rise, throw my shoulders back and salute them.

Hotshot's brow hikes. "Are you selling something?"

Oh, do I look that cheap in my corduroys? "No," I say in a small voice.

"Want donations?"

"Huh? No, no, I saw you on TV yesterday and wish to volunteer."

He looks me over, sneering. "Aren't you a few decades too late to enlist?"

My shoulders slump. Bah, age jokes, always with the age jokes. "What? I have as much right to join the force as you," I say testily.

He crosses his arms, his eyes steeling. "Okay, give me twenty."

I blink on repeat, rubbing the nape of my neck. Does he want money or more time? "Eh?"

"Twenty push-ups, you fool."

My chest draws taut. When did I last manage five? "Twenty?"

Hotshot and his cronies are snickering while I gingerly squat to outstretch my limbs over the icy floor. Goddammit, why can't I run into reasonable people for a change?

One, ugh. Two, ugh. My arms wobble worse than dad's old jalopy.

Three, ugh. Four, ow. I wince as my back screams from the strain.

Five, ugh…

I collapse to the floor spread-eagled and panting, while they double up leaning on each other's shoulders, mirthfully braying.

Hotshot holds his gut, taking in and blowing out a lungful to recover his breath. "Get it now, uncle? Firefighting is tough work. Should we install an elevator for you on the truck? Go volunteer as a crossing guard."

Ba-dum-tss! A bucket of alcohol to a gunshot wound.

I bound to my feet, scowling. "Okay, how do I sign up? And don't play the pope with me. I bet city officials would love to hear of your many unwritten rules."

Hotshot's chest puffs out, his sneer renewing. "Hah. You don't have a case."

My lips show an evil grin. This dimwit doesn't know muckraking is my superpower. "I don't need one, bro. I just need to make enough noise."

Hotshot flinches for a beat before he turns away, waving a dismissive hand. "Fine, fine. You have a week. If you can jog a mile and do the push-ups, you're in on probation. Now get out."

Bah, stupid ride, always brings me pain. Late afternoon the next day, I'm circling the vast muddy lake in the leafy Eco-park near my place, my ratty sneakers shambling over its dirt track. Neat rows of low bushy shrubs oversee my masochism, my limbs melting into unset jelly, my heart ba-dump-ba-dumping to a silent dance track.

A soft gusty breeze is nicking my face, stinging my eyes; magnifying the want to barf and blow my nose together every half-mile. Then it finally approaches, the bosky fence hemming the exit, and I croak a hallelujah. For today, at least, the torture ends.

Who are these three? I decelerate to a standstill, drawing heavy breaths, while they blab with their backs turned. Backpacks and hoodies over skinny jeans.

College kids? What're they doing here? Shouldn't they be loafing in a mall somewhere? Wait, wait, didn't I read in the paper yesterday that Ipoh thugs now dress trendily to scam unsuspecting targets? Curses.

Stooping, I shakily fumble inside my sneaker to scoop out a spiky gray pebble and flick it away. The only other jogger around is an exclamation mark in the distance, and if he deduces they're thugs, he'll doubtless spin round and sprint away.

Argh, man up, Holliday. What can they possibly steal from you? Maybe they're here to birdwatch, or they're birdbrains. Either way, stop overreacting. You're likely low on blood sugar, so get going and grab a candy bar on the way home.

I'm stretching from side to side to calm my nerves. Okay, on the off chance they're criminals posing as students, the key is to act unconcerned. I'll trot past them without hellos and hit top speed from there.

The wiry fellow in the blue hoodie glimpses over his shoulder and meets my stare. And though he's cheerily waving a forked pine twig, and his massive snout you could spot from the moon, it's the dark swooshy scar on his cheek that chills my fingers into ice cubes. Uh-oh. There are only two ways to get that scar, and I doubt his father does experimental surgery.

Panic pulls me into its irresistible straightjacket, flooding my mind with a mishmash of distressing scenarios, each one ending with me tied to a tree in my birthday suit. My only choice is to flee downslope, unless he's a track star, in which case I'm screwed.

I wheel round and shift into a canter, behind me Snouty's footsteps thudding faster and faster. Goddammit, I'm too drained to dash. Aside from the washed-out ten bucks in my wallet, what can I present these fiends to keep my pinkies?

"Excuse me, sir," a nasally voice hollers. "Can you please help us?"

Oh, when did the cretins gain manners? I break off mid-stride and face him, bristling. "What, what's your problem?"

Snouty pulls up a few feet from me, wearing a guilty smile

while stroking his mussy mop-top hair. "Sorry to startle you, sir, but we'd really appreciate your cooperation."

His friends bumble to his side, bearing the same apologetic faces. My cooperation? That's how they're robbing people now? Jeez, how low have Ipoh crooks sunk in my lifetime?

My foot briskly taps the gravel as I'm frowning at them. "What's your game?"

Snouty flaps his hands to signal I misread them. He explains they're college kids out on assignment, fishing for comments on city stories. "Nobody has time for us. We'll fail the course at this rate," he says, pouting.

My head tips skyward and I let out a slow, deep breath. Ah failure, my most ignoble friend. We meet once more through your latest prey. Helping others, huh? Is this my true calling in life?

"Alright, I'll help," I say, sighting their simpers. "But don't you dare make me look stupid, okay?"

Snouty eagerly nods, and at once they jump into the job. While his comrades are fidgeting with their handheld video camera, he guides me from spot to spot foregrounding the lake.

Butterflies, a battalion of them, are fluttering in my tummy as I recollect my long-lost personable smile while fussily running a hand through my sparse hair.

Satisfied at last, Snouty darts back to his friends behind the camera. "Action!" he says, with a snappy flourish of his twig, before aping a newscaster's gravitas. "Sir, what do you think of the city swapping crossing guards for traffic robots in a year's time?"

"W-what? Who told you that?" I ask, gawking at him.

"It's everywhere on the news. You didn't know?"

My heartbeat throbs louder in my ears while I wring my hands many shades of blue. Curses, how could I? Last night those morons at the diner kept the TV channel to insipid soaps. "I just know they slashed my work hours."

"You're a—"

"Two decades and counting."

They trade shocked looks. "Wow. What is your opinion?" Snouty asks.

My balled fists tremble, and my cheeks must be redder than a pot roast. Goddammit, the cosmic joker strikes again.

"It's an abomination," I say, rising on my tiptoes, wagging my finger at the camera. "A crosswalk is no place for glorified tin cans. No, sir, my job requires a human touch. We are both shrinks and public servants."

My rant startles them briefly, and they pull away a step. Snouty regains his composure first, puckering his lips to thereon balance the twig. "You don't say."

The crazed bobcat in me sets free, and my arms are flailing. "How will a robot sense someone had an awful day and needs compassion? That a young child didn't sleep enough and could space out—"

I face-palm, lightly shaking my head, a mirthless chuckle escaping me. Hah, who knew? Two decades on, even a wart of a job becomes you. How ridiculous.

Snouty and friends break into golf claps and I offer them a weak smile. Pity you're the only people who care.

I turn away from them, pulling back angry tears, the infinite winding dirt-track painfully symbolic of my plight. "Now excuse me, I have to run again."

Will I soon become obsolete? Another scrap of the past set aflame to welcome the future?

Dad's favorite explanation for my mediocre life is I'm a serial quitter. Bah, what does the lunatic know? Life's easy when you don't dream and are perfectly happy plodding through a humdrum existence. And it's much easier to pontificate from your high horse when the rub of the green is spilling your way. I can't do the former, and the latter has always eluded me. Doubtless the last five days were a total nightmare, but at least I made it. Despite my laundry list of flaws and failings, I'm still trying.

Yes, I have every right to twirl before this full-length mirror in my spanking jumpsuit. Yeah, the color black doesn't flatter only the pale ghouls. It's incredible what a desperate man can do when he's knees deep in a giant flushing toilet.

Beaming, I meticulously fasten the chin strap of my white hard hat, then tuck the banded goggles above its brim. Aside from me, in the windowless and dank locker-room lined with red doorless closets, other rookies are climbing into their fireproof gear and making small talk.

Hotshot barges in that moment and starts barking orders: "Okay, team. We got a tip-off for ten blocks south on the top floor. A small fire. You noobs follow protocol and don't disappoint me."

He throws me a pointed look, to which I dutifully nod, before sticking my tongue out the instant the killjoy shifts toward the door.

The sermon in my head starts anew. Holliday, Holliday, don't mind him, we did good. Kept our wrath in check on training day when we yearned to rip his throat out, but it's okay for we have the memory of an elephant. Someday, he'll race into a raging blaze and we'll padlock the exit. He-he, that'll force superman to learn to fly in forty pounds of gear.

Minutes later, its sirens ablare, our fire truck is hurtling through the long afternoon shadows on Ipoh's dusty potholed roads. Though the bemused smiles of my makeshift comrades are visible in the side-view mirror, I insist on leaning off the ladder, one gloved bony hand clutching the top rail.

Yikes! Our kamikaze driver makes another hairpin turn at top gear that nearly frees my grip and slings me into a lamppost. Does he do death-defying stunts in the local motordrome? Deep breaths, Holliday. I'm okay, everything's okay. My hat's whistling in the toasty wind, and my lips are humming the same sprightly tune.

The truck soon brings up before a row of alabaster-and-gray shop-houses hemmed between a scrapyard and fields of wild sugarcane. I leap off, unhook one end of the fire hose, and scurry to find the nearest hydrant; my huge grin refusing to contain. At long last, I'm a hero.

Of my two teammates, one shoots up the truck to orient the ladder, while the other zips inside the building to scout the blaze. My pulse is galloping when I return to the truck, rocking on my feet next to the pump panel, awaiting news on the poor saps we'll save today.

The scout waddles out the building and toward us, shrugging. "Nothing. The tenants say they didn't call anyone."

My face scrunches up at the update. "The hell? Does Hotshot get his tips from angel radio?"

"Cut," someone yells rightward, and right after, a trio in camouflage tees emerge from behind the tangled brushes hugging the shop-houses and are loping toward the fire truck.

One of them cradles a video camera to his chest, and its sight boils my blood. Snouty and his band of boneheads. Curses, curses.

"Excellent job, guys," Snouty says, swishing his twig for effect. "We never thought volunteers could respond to a fire with such speed."

I step toward him, glowering. "What're you doing?"

He peers at me overlong, and then his hand flies to his heart. "It's you, sir! Why, your comments that day really opened our eyes. There's so much injustice everywhere, which is why we became citizen journalists to better serve Ipoh," he says brightly.

Before I can unpack my encyclopedia of acid-dipped condemnations, he segues into a lengthy and entirely bonkers monologue on civil rights, at which point the other firefighters' questioning stares bore into me as a hail of lead.

I'm pretending to find a gravelly pattern on the blacktop, flushing and gritting my teeth. Again, I effing did it again. Shoot me in the nuts now. Keep helping others, Holliday, why don't you? If only I could tape sticks of dynamite to this busybody's face and push him into an open sewer.

Snouty's lecture continues, his gestures elastic as if he were spinning yarn. "We faked the fire because we had to verify your response times. People want to know where their tax money goes…"

I steal back to the panel and unwind the hose with deft turns. "…confident local news will pay us to uncover the flaws in emergency services. Not to compare virtues, but I believe we're the real-life Watchmen. You know, the superhero movie?"

The hose raises to my ribs, and I lock it underarm when unscrewing the chrysanthemum-shaped faucet.

Snouty glances to me and forthwith the whites of his eyes overwhelm his irises.

"No, bro. You are dead men," I say, before high-pressure water gushes through the hose to smash into the trio, launching them backward in the air.

Their camera joins them on the asphalt a beat later, cracking open as a plastic omelet with bits of metal and multicolored wires sticking out.

They stagger to their feet shell-shocked, scoop its carcass and dash toward the brushes. Snouty twists his torso mid-sprint, his snapped twig waggling at me. "We'll be back," he shrieks.

Perfect, I'll collect dynamite sticks and machetes for the occasion. "Now we're even," I say, mic-dropping the hose.

The scout reaches to coil it, groaning. "You're a real handful, you know that? Wait till the boss hears of this." The other one just shakes his head and cranks in the ladder.

I pay them no mind, instead smacking together my glorified oven mitts to release my lingering rage. Bah, this was my time to win, you peasants. You're lucky I'm still searching for Earth's self-destruct button.

The fire truck's driver-side door clunks open and slams. "That wasn't very nice," he says, and at once I gasp. What the eff? Is this his doing?

Yaya slaps on his newsboy cap, squirming in his black jumpsuit as though it's crawling with ants. "Been a while," he says, skipping up to me.

My nostrils aflare, I yank off my hat and angrily jab it in his direction. "What's wrong with you?"

He curls the corkscrews in his beard, unperturbed. "Do you believe in God?"

A storm of cusses swells inside me. "Of course. I can't have ruined my life by myself, you stupid geezer."

"Touché," Yaya says, snickering.

"Hey, you dropped something," the scout interrupts, motioning to a paper scrap by my boots.

I shoot Yaya a nasty look while crouching to retrieve the scrap. It's the same as before, the dimensions of a tea-coaster, though today it carries a crude sketch of two bent trees.

"Is this going anywhere? These random drawings and the dots and lines?" I ask, glaring at him.

Yaya tut-tuts, his finger swinging to-and-fro as a pendulum. "The real question, son, is can you become the man you pretend to be?"

Argh, more riddles. "What the hell is your problem?" I spit back.

"He-he, don't always be rushing," he says, whirling round and disappearing behind the truck.

The scout walks up to me. "Um, is he going to drive us back?"

I grimly rest my fist on his shoulder. "He can only drive us off a cliff. Best start walking."

⌘

— Week Three —

Clumsy Cupid

Life, I conclude, is a series of choices, each one a precise level of ludicrous, so the best we can hope for is choosing the lesser evil. For instance, there's the clever marketing guys who coined Malaysia a tropical paradise. Now, when I find them, and oh yes, I will, they'll choose between a bullet to the knee and a karate chop to the kisser. Either way, those unrepentant scammers will discover a world of pain.

My legs are beating as a wet dog to unload the water swashing round in my thin-soled loafers. Ahead, the crosswalk pools with rainwater from the heavy monsoon; in murky wavelets lapping against my socks each time I venture forward to stop traffic. Curses.

Shivering, I pull the hood of my faded raincoat tighter over my scalp and check the fogged-up dial of my cheap digital watch. Argh, another twenty minutes before I can stop playing an old crone from a Disney flop and nip to the nearest diner for a cup of steaming chocolate malt.

My rump sets on the sidewalk and I prop my weather-beaten traffic lollipop between my thighs. Leftward of me, the stoplight pulses yellow again, my foot bouncing in time with its blinks.

Please Lord, for once let my shift end with no more busybodies wishing to cross the road. Stupid me, why do I never qualify for sick leaves? Tomorrow I should accost a stranger nursing a wicked flu and steal their snot to smear over my face. Beats risking pneumonia every day, if not slipping on slick and breaking my uninsured leg.

Then my bleary eyes flash wide open, and I bolt to my feet. The stoplight's showing red, yet from the far edge of the crosswalk, a pair of stilettos under a tent-size umbrella are strolling over the zebra lines.

I fumble inside the raincoat for my whistle, and promptly empty my lungs into its mouthpiece, yet Heels clacks onward without care. My lips curl in disgust. What is this dolt doing? Okay, time for the emergency protocol.

I'm pogoing on my feet while furiously waving the lollipop, aping a horny chimp, but again she notices not. Instead, Heels is weaving through the honking cars and mopeds with the finesse of a Frogger champion.

My arms limply fall to my sides. Curses, is she deaf, blind and stupid? "What are you doing?" I ask, scowling, when Heels enters spitting distance.

Her umbrella tilts backward to expose a woman in trendy wear sporting mascara so thick she must own a coal mine. Heels gives me a once-over, sneering. "Why do you small-town hillbillies have such short walking times, huh? Do they reflect your puny attention spans?"

Then she brushes past me, the arrowhead tips of her umbrella carving thin grooves on my cheek. I touch my face, speechless, grimacing at her buxom profile. You sassy sow, I hope your stilettos snap and shove you before a distracted truck driver. Bah, you remind me so much of dad's side of the family I'd happily be that driver.

My pants are vibrating without pause. I slip out my cellphone, soughing, and over its grainy screen I flatten the lollipop. My lips at once form a mirthless smile. Ah, the devil arises from his slumber. Why's the old coot messaging me?

No sooner does my finger skate over the screen that I break into a flood tide of swears. No effing way. Impossible, impossible. I can't be right, I'm never right. The lollipop clunks against the walkway when the line connects.

"Dad. The photo. Who is she?"

Strange throaty noises greet me from the other end of the line and a cuss catches in my throat. Is he gargling or gagging this time? Humph, what's with this mad ritual whenever I call?

"Oh, it's you," the distant reedy voice says. "Don't you remember your cousin from KL?"

Please, God, let it be a lookalike. "Tell me she's not in town."

"Well, yes, why text you otherwise? To rejoice at your absent success?" Dad says, chuckling.

My shoulders hump and I pinch the bridge of my nose. Age plainly hasn't dulled his gift for savaging my self-esteem. Long ago, I imagine his clan skinned dragons for a living.

"So, be a good boy and show her around tomorrow, won't you?"

My scorn finds speech as a grunt. "No, thanks. Met the grouch in passing today. I don't need the humiliation."

Dad clucks disapprovingly. "Humiliation? You need self-respect for that, son." His tone grows smug. "She's a corporate big shot who needn't sneeze at you. Do yourself this favor, yes? Maybe she'll land you a better gig or something."

My eyes squeeze shut as I'm rubbing my forehead in slow circular strokes. Without fail, every damn time, he belittles me. It's a shame no one ever kidnapped me as a kid, even when I offered my piggy bank to those shady beggars outside school. "Fine, fine, one night and that's it."

"Good, good, I'll send you her number," Dad says cheerily. Then his voice dips to a whisper, as if he's sharing state secrets.

"Unbelievable as it sounds, she's still single. I know God shafted you in the looks department, but women can be very naive. What's the harm? It's obvious you could do no worse."

"Goodbye." Beep.

I wilt to the pavement and zoom into Heels's picture. Her sloe-eyed smile and dainty nose aren't unattractive, but that personality needs industrial strength bleach. If nothing else, her photo proves even cretins can affect charm when necessary. Hmm, when last did I dine with a woman outside those dreary work picnics?

The little man inside my head yawns. Holliday, Holliday, we should just feign death, for dining with her is a recipe for disaster. Your pride is running on fumes as is, and in case you forget, you can't replenish it at a gas pump.

The now dark screen mirrors my glum countenance. "What if Yaya's testing me again, huh? I bail out now and there's no coming back."

Silence.

A part of me demands I burst into maniacal laughter; a stark blackout sets in the rest.

My word, those Himalayan heaps of coconut milk and sugar. How in blazes does anyone stay thin in this city? Must be the water, or the tapeworms. Are they in such a rush to die early?

Every day, of every year, of every decade, the airy floodlit food court packs with Ipoh's gastric wonders, who throng its hole-in-the-wall hawkers rowing the plaza, drifting from one stall to another as scent hounds hunting for the most unwholesome fare.

I'm drumming on the disklike fiberglass table, my shakes syncing with the throbbing in my ears. She's late; surprise, surprise. Heels, I'm willing to bet, believes she's performing charity by indulging the family disaster.

Well, boohoo, I'm sorry I'm not a lawyer or a high-powered cop. None of you had my father for a dad.

Then I'm fidgeting with the floppy lapels of my jacket and its raveling sleeves. Dry-cleaning the antique did little good, though it won't matter if her self-righteousness sets it on fire. Hell, I might burn to a cinder first. Well, Holliday, consider tonight a success if afterward you don't rush home to curl up in a corner and bawl your eyes out.

A distinct clicking sound distracts me. Heels is sashaying over the well-trodden discolored tiles, her shades tucked over her forehead, her wavy locks now bunched together in a twisted topknot. She blankly glances round at the patrons until she sights me and her expression steels. I rise, my palm wiping across my clammy neck. This was a terrible, terrible idea.

Heels drops her capacious handbag on the tabletop and lowers onto a stool opposite me. "Where were your manners yesterday? And don't bother ordering," she declares with a dismissive flourish.

Though I'm simpering, my fist clenches from the feverish impulse to meet her flesh. "Glad you could make it."

She sets her elbows on the counter and beholds me with a bemused stare. "You know, it always puzzles me why people spend their entire lives in the boonies. Don't you want a better life?"

Great, another snob from the mighty concrete jungle. It's a runaway epidemic with these loons. I manage a strained laugh. "Ipoh is home, I guess."

Heels bears a sly grin. "Well, some people call mud huts home too."

The knuckles on my balled fist are turning white, but then the food she ordered arrives, and we're both gaping at the spread: her bright-eyed, me dumbstruck.

One right after the other, bustling servers plate our table with enough sticky rice, and soupy stew, and toothpick-thin meat skewers to end world hunger.

Heels right away dispenses with her holier-than-thou act, now that her ornately painted nails are clawing at the skewers, and she's scarfing the meat with ogreish etiquette.

I squirm on my stool, the metal edges of my wallet pointedly stabbing my backside. Does she plan to pay? Curses, I should have brought along my dish-washing gloves. What now? Should I excuse myself to go to the toilet and split?

Heels pulls away from the skewers, stifling a burp, only to resume her takedown of me while sputtering grains of rice that gather on my lap. "If I'm honest, it'd be hard for you to find work there. I mean, there's so much automation and you're too old for manual labor, right?"

I ignore the grains and fixedly nibble on a skewer before my fury finds shape as an uppercut. Sadists, every one of them.

After scouring high and low, it's my firm belief there's not a decent man, woman, or child in dad's family tree.

Something furry brushes against me and I flinch, swatting my leg. Her brow hikes to complete her quizzical look.

"Are you having a seizure?"

"No," I say, my gaze darting between her and the floor. "You were saying?"

She doesn't need my encouragement. As I suspect, Heels is far too self-absorbed to probe further. Now she's inhaling spoonfuls of stew one after the other, only breaking to impress upon me in great detail the glories of big city life, her peepers throughout twinkling with pride.

I chime in now and again with judicious nods and you-don't-says, always peeking under our table where three white-and-orange kittens are grooming their fuzzy whiskers, and throwing me cool half-lidded looks.

My hand cups over my knee to curb the urge to spring a swift kick. The sneaky little scalawags, they're up to no good. But if I undertake to chase them away, Heels might consider me cruel, and I daren't present her more reasons to bully me.

Okay, Holliday, endure it, for this nightmare's end is nigh.

I reach my fork for the few remaining morsels of rice. Try to make the best of this bind, why don't you? Heels must have her good points, everybody does. "So, how come you're still single? Surely you have many suitors?"

Heels perks up at the compliment and fakes a sigh. "Men today are so boring. Total lack of ambition. There's you, for example. Can you really blame a girl for not settling?"

"Uh-huh," I say, the fork on its own training at her fleshy neck.

Curses, why can't people ever rise to my meager expectations of them? Hmm, I wonder if her left or right jowl will bleed faster.

Shadows zip by my ear and straightaway the tabletop clatters. I jerk backward, unable to contain a yelp.

The treacherous tabbies are skittering round the plates as seasoned acrobats, snapping up the meat skewers before launching in different directions.

Heels screams, and right after, my skin burns. Her eyes are following the kittens making their grand escape, while she clings to a ceramic bowl that hitherto filled with hot soy milk.

Frowning, I pluck the gooey grains of barley off my forehead and cheeks, and then towel them with my hankie. This night keeps getting better and better. What's the encore? A black cloud that only rains on me?

"Ugh, kittens. They're such horrible little devils," she says, wrinkling her nose and replacing the bowl on the table.

The infernal pusses are feasting under a metal cooking grill in eyeshot, and I yearn for their company. Right now, I'll gladly partake of dinner with a blind, one-legged mongoose. Anyone but her.

"Pity they have no taste for human flesh," I mutter to myself.

Heels folds her arms below her bosom, pouting and glancing round the court. "Where's the ATM here? How do people survive in this dump?"

My heart lightens into a fluffy chapati. Praise the Lord, does she mean to pay for dinner? And here I was fretting I'd need to pawn my kidneys. "It's only a few blocks away," I say, glowing. "Give me your card and I'll be back in a jiffy."

She pats her handbag, scoffing at my suggestion. "No need. Your dad warned me, so I'm carrying a chunk of cash. Bless that man, he's a veritable saint."

The memory of the soy milk stings my face anew like a disfiguring old war wound. Saint? SAINT? Next, she'll start praising Satan. No, I cannot be indebted to this horrible woman. If I have to scrub dishes till morning to cover for the meal, so be it.

"Should go pay," I mumble, sliding off the stool.

Heels is busy glaring at something behind me. Wow, is there no end to things that annoy her? I glimpse over my shoulder to sight plastic crackling inches from my nose and forthwith squeal and jump aside from the figure.

Oh, the mute old uncle. His crinkly visage curves into a kind smile as he's tapping the laminated sign dangling round his collar. Goddammit, he still has the nasty habit of sneaking up on you.

I seat myself, taking deep breaths to calm my rattling pulse. "It's okay, he's harmless."

Crinkles is swishing round packs of pocket tissues and touching his sign.

My head solemnly shakes before I return to Heels's dirty look. No sense scrubbing dishes for an extra hour, though I've always admired his quiet dignity. Next time, maybe, when I'm not paying for the entire village.

"Tell him to leave. He gives me the creeps," she says sharply.

"He will, he will."

No sooner do I make that pronouncement that his arm flashes past me and Heels shrieks.

A beat later, Crinkles is dashing through the aisles clutching her handbag, knocking over servers and diners alike.

Heels cups her hands round her mouth and yells, "thief."

Then, her bosom heaving, she shoots me an icy stare. "What are you waiting for, fool? Get it back."

My lips pinch together and a dull ache builds in my limbs. Ack, why must I? Why did the crackpot choose today to pull this stunt? He should've just knifed me in the back and spat on my corpse.

I wearily arise, sulking, and shuffle after the uncle who's blitzing through the court at Usain Bolt's speed. Curses, he sure fooled me with the old man act. Of everyone present, am I the only one with the word chump stamped on my forehead?

Twice I must detour round a traffic jam of slaphappy geriatrics and then hop over the outstretched legs of ill-mannered runts. And hard though I try, their sniggers drill into my ears, and reddening, I start into a canter.

Soon after, I lumber out the plaza into the light-and-shade parking lot, squinting left and right. I should skin Crinkles alive for adding to my misery, but he could be streets away with his lead. Bah, this chase is futile.

Rightward, a silhouette catches my eye. It's him, a stone's throw away, sitting on a bumper block in the first row of cars, feeding the thieving kittens a fistful of rice.

I frisk my pants for a weapon, one I can use to gouge out his peepers, but besides my wallet there's only a rusty paper clip or two. That's okay, I'll wallop him black-and-blue with my shoe.

Crinkles must sense my bloodlust as I'm storming toward him, for he raises his veiny hand to signal I stop.

I abide, though every sinew in my body strains to hollow out his insides and stuff them with tissues. The geezer better claim a divine explanation for his crime, or else.

He reaches behind him to produce Heels's handbag, and promptly overturns it so an assortment of bottles and tubes clap against the asphalt, as does a fat wad of cash tied with elastic bands. Aha! It goes against my principles to attack the elderly, but there's none more deserving than him.

"For a thief, you're an actual idiot," I say, lifting a leg to slip off my shoe.

Unshaken by my threat, he stoops to grab the cash and holds it toward me. Then he's thumbing through the bills and my breath hitches.

Two five-dollar bills slot at the top and tail while the rest are worthless scraps. I double over, grasping my kneecaps. Un-effing-believable, I've been…

"She duped you, son," Crinkles says in a low, cultured voice.

Light footsteps near me and halt. "Here's fifty bucks to help with the check," he says, slipping money into my coat pocket and pushing the handbag into my lap.

"W-wait, you can speak?" I ask, straightening.

Crinkles smirks in response. "How perceptive. The quick version is I'm a novelist, and what better way to study human nature than sell something nobody wants?"

My mind reels from the one-two punch of recent bombshells. "But why steal the handbag?"

He hoists the kittens to cradle them in his arms. "Thought I'd help you in setting her straight. See too many of her stripe nowadays." Then he's moseying toward the back rows, briefly waving his goodbye. "Think of me as your good karma."

My ticker thuds louder in my ribs. Good karma? Me? Is that even possible? "The cops," I exclaim. "They'll be here soon and people know you."

Crinkles looks back with a wry grin. "Do they now?"

In profile, Heels's pressed lips and sharp crow's feet make her appear a poisonous toad, but her tantrums no longer concern me. I march back to our table after settling the tab and thereon plunk her handbag.

"Let's take a stroll," I say, my thumb pointing to the slim path that coils along the length of the court.

Her face blanches for a beat, and though she's speechless, her sneer stays true as a stuck-up pro's should. I face away and start walking.

"Fine, what do you want?" she snaps, clumping up to me. "Don't expect me to reward you. I told you to shoo away the crook."

"He's no crook."

Heels breaks her stride and makes the teapot pose. "So, where did my cash go? You brought back worthless scraps, moron. I ought to call the cops on you."

Unmoved, I step in and hold her gaze. "Funny, never saw you check."

Heels's eyes grow wide, her fingertips touching her parted lips. Then she blushes and looks away.

The proverbial black cloud is looming overhead, ready to pepper me with speary icicles. Yep, I'm a chump. "I'll leave now. Please tell me the car is yours at least."

I don't wait for her answer, yet to my astonishment she's following me. We weave through columns of obscenely parked cars, and past the parking lot's weedy rim to where my bicycle leans against a bowed palm tree.

I sheepishly flick her a two-finger salute. "Be seeing you."

Heels's hand places on my distant arm, her eyes large and glossy. "Why did you take me aside? You could've embarrassed me in front of everyone and had your revenge."

Great question. Is it because I see mother in her someway? But I remember so little…argh, stop it, Holliday. What's wrong with you? Stop bringing up memories that ache your heart.

I pull away from her to raise the bicycle upright, my hands atremble. "I may not be Shah Rukh Khan, but neither am I the ill-mannered baboon your family believes me to be."

Heels roots to her spot when I swing atop the saddle. "Can we meet next time I'm in town?" she hollers as I'm pedaling upslope onto the gold-lit road.

Though I know not to grin, I can't help it. Ah, Holliday, it's an interesting dream. If there is…if we have a next time, you needn't try so hard to sabotage it. No one's perfect, and should an exception exist, it'd never be you.

"Depends," I say, curving behind a gather of bark cloth trees. "Do you eat pot noodles?"

Minutes later, my tummy is somersaulting, and I ease up by the curb to scan across the road for a bodega among the iridescent shop-houses. Wish I'd eaten more, but what to do? Heels must've been starving. Thank heavens she only ordered the cheap stuff. Speaking of which, I should find Crinkles and return his money.

I'm wrestling with the coat's pocket lining to pull out the cash, grunting, the bicycle tottering in sync with my struggle. Why, why are the saddles perched so high on these ancient oddballs? The folded bills pop out asudden, evading my grasp and flopping onto the asphalt, and shoulder first I follow.

I snap upright and blow out a lungful. Splendid, no guffawing witnesses for once. Now, where's the cash? Hmm, five ten-dollar bills and…

Breathless, I rush to the curbstone, to the humped streetlight to pitch the paper cut as a tea-coaster under its tungsten glow. Again, a duo of dots interrupting a straight line, while on its flip side the spidery cursive reads: *seek and ye shall find.*

In that moment, the sheer absurdity of my quest overwhelms me, and I throw back my head and explode into unhinged laughter. Two cosmic jokers in one universe, or are they the same? Curses, I'm screwed. Unquestionably screwed.

⌘

The Other Foot

Me and Ipoh traffic have a peculiar relationship. Most days, the whooshing cars, the whizzing mopeds, the whirring bicycles, and the unceasing pedestrian prattle meld into a tuneless wall of sound that my brain adroitly ignores.

Other days, today particularly, even the loose chain-ring bolts on an old auntie's bicycle have me reaching for my traffic lollipop to split open her head. Hey, I'm not at fault here. After a streak of sleepless nights, any sane human will be as high-strung as a cricket fleeing insect repellent.

Tsk-tsk, says the annoying fellow in my head. Holliday, Holliday, you spineless jellyfish. Why do you allow those street racing pests to zip and zoom in the dead of night and ruin our repose? Are you a man or a mongoose? Find a boot with the heft of a flatbed trailer and squish them ASAP.

Yawn. Fair point for I direly need sleep the length of Rip Van Winkle's. Pity the liquor in this town takes after horse tinkle, or I'd drink myself into oblivion.

It's essential I scheme a solution to my predicament, but what? My stupor is at a point where planning beyond the basic biological functions brings on a violent migraine.

Sigh, still an hour to go before the clock strikes lunch and I'm home free. I'm propping upright against a tombstone, or at least that's how the bronzed steel of the stoplight pole feels to my spine. And inch by inch, the lollipop slips closer to the sidewalk from my slackening grip.

My bloodshot eyes beg me to leave them sealed, and yet I must now and again glimpse ahead, my fingers crossed no jaywalkers crush into roadkill today. And should they achieve such, they'll peel themselves off the asphalt and call a taxi to the funeral parlor. Nope, don't expect unappreciated diligence from me this week.

And don't you uppity fools pooh-pooh me. I pride myself on playing the dutiful drone at work, always have. Yet I cannot deny only a dribble of adrenaline keeps in my body, and that I need to drag myself home and collapse into bed.

Someone is shouting? Why? "Oi, you blind?" the voice says before exploding into cusses.

My eyelids creak open. At the far side of the crosswalk, a mousy woman wearing fat-rimmed spectacles is thrashing her arms high and low as if she's bracing to take flight. Beside her, a throng of grumpy walkers are shaking their heads, throwing me dirty looks.

Goddammit, what energy bars do these people eat for breakfast? I wearily clasp the lollipop and plod ahead to stop traffic.

Soon they're bustling across the zebra lines, their frigid stares lasering into my back, and in return my palms break a sweat.

It's okay, Holliday, let them call the agency and complain to their heart's content. It's not as though you're up for promotion in this lifetime.

The mousy woman, though, is a genuine salt-of-the-earth busybody. She halts next to me and crosses her arms, scorn dripping from her every pore.

No sense escalating the issue, not in my condition. More and more women practice karate nowadays, I hear, and it's the petite ones who spell the most trouble. My face gathers into a simper. "Sorry, it's the damned weather. Made me lose focus."

Her eyes shrink to slits. "Lazy people like you sicken me. When will you stop shaming this great country, huh?" Then she huffs away while an arctic chill benumbs my bones.

The lollipop sets against my humped shoulder as I slouch back to the walkway. Why, why does no one recall the time I volunteered for double shifts outside the stadium so these loons could watch their precious team play?

Or when those hyperactive toddlers waded into rush-hour traffic and I dashed in to save them at great peril to myself? Bah, screw these ingrates.

My slacks are agitating from mechanical vibrations. Hmm, an unknown phone number. Is it someone from the security agency checking on me incognito? Nah, even if the woman complained, they'd never be this efficient.

"Mr. Holliday?" the curt voice on the phone asks.

"Yes?"

Pages flip while the man is muttering to himself, and I swallow to ease the lump in my esophagus. Is he calling from city hall? Was it not last night I overheard someone at the diner mention Ipoh was introducing new taxes?

Curses, they won't add bicycles to the road tax bracket, right? "You still there? I'm calling from the studio. You wished to audition for the walk-on part, right?"

Hallelujah, they called! I press the phone tighter over my ear. "Yes, yes, correct."

"Good, you're on in three days. Around noon. Don't be late, the role could grow to main cast."

My face bears a loopy grin. "Understood, sir. Thank you."

I take a knee on the sidewalk, twice pumping the lollipop in the air. Took these people long enough. You'd think they were building the pyramids.

An invisible needle instantly pricks my happy balloon. Ah, crap, those damn street racers. My arms slump to my sides, and I sag to the pavement. If I sleepwalk to the audition, the only studio in town will blacklist me forever.

The lollipop places flat on my lap, and I studiously pick at its flaking paint. Earmuffs don't work. Without proof, I can't go to the cops, and my phone takes awful video without distinction. Can't afford a new one either. Argh, should I book a budget motel for that night? Move out?

My lips thin into a slash and my fingernails bite into my palms. Stop it, Holliday, don't be absurd. Why should my wallet empty for someone else's villainy? No, I should investigate posthaste. At least one ne'er-do-well in my neighborhood must know these parasites. No, no more mister-nice-mongoose.

Well, scratch that plan. It's a rare day when I can keep my promises to myself, and today's not one of them. The bicycle is bucketing from my tired strokes when I wind into my skinny dead-end street, at which point I don't doubt a sloth in medieval armor could pedal faster than me.

Gliding past the row of gable-roofed houses, both deluxe and dilapidated, it strikes me that sleuthing in my state is a terrible idea. Another restless night and I'll likely go on a murderous shooting spree. Yes, it's best I get a brief shut-eye first.

Hmm, who's that? I lean forward on the handlebar, squinting. Ahead, by the road's paved shoulder bordering the greenbelt, a mohawked youth is gunning a blue sports bike with his face glued to its meter panel, raising a god-awful racket.

My teeth bare on their own. Why, it's that cheeky punk **from five houses up who routinely throws me death stares. I** jam the handbrakes, scowling. Hold on, is he one of those deadbeats ruining my life?

A prodigious yawn overcomes me and I smack my lips, leaning over to knead my sore calves. Curses, I'm running on empty, but a quick chat won't hurt. If nothing else, I'll strike public disorder from his list of mental defects. Plus, knowing his kind, he won't chase after me while the sun's still out.

My bicycle glides up to him, and I plant both feet on the blacktop. His sunken, angular features always give me the willies. "How's it going, bro?" I say with forced cheer.

"All good, gramps," he says, his fingers tweaking his prickly hair styled as a skunk.

Swears as a roaring rapid race to my lips, but I hold steady. Bah, must these morons always peg me for a mossback? "Think you guys can move your midnight joyride elsewhere? Some of us have to wake early, you know."

Skunky coldly stares in reply, now revving his bike's engine to ear-splitting decibels. "You see anyone else complaining?"

Aha, he is part of the gang. "That's not the point," I say, wagging my finger at him. "You can't make all that noise after midnight. I have rights, you know, and what you're doing is illegal, anyway."

Skunky surveys me with a disdain that suggests I'm the fresh muck on his mudguard. "Gramps, can't you see you're the problem? You've forgotten how to have fun, so you want to kill it for everyone else too. Why don't you just find a coffin and start practicing, no?"

My hand furiously scrubs over my face. Again, again with the gramps nonsense. "That's it, insolent brat," I bark, sitting up in the saddle and squaring my shoulders. "I'm done, so done, being civil with you. Clearly I should speak to your unfortunate parents."

Skunky howls obscenely as a tickled hyena. "Good luck with that, gramps."

Argh, I hope you skid into a ditch. I'm glowering at him while storming across the road to his bespoke slatted steel gate, whereupon I knock out the bicycle stand and at once pummel the doorbell that makes a cuckoo sound. How apt. Before long, a tall professorial man with a toadish mouth drifts toward me. Must be the rich father. Thank God for sane adults.

Toady stays silent through my rant, staring into space while caressing his wispy goatee. Then he good-naturedly shrugs. "Well, nobody has ever complained before, and I confess I snooze like the dead. I promise I'll talk to him, but the lad does his own thing, you know?"

Wow, what's wrong with this family? Why do I always find myself among unreasonable fiends? I ditch my incredulous look after spinning round and straddling my bicycle to head home.

And though I fight the impulse, my gaze wanders toward Skunky, who's flashing me two spindly middle fingers and smirking.

Goddammit, God-effing-dammit. My nostrils are flaring into limes and an intense bloodlust clouds my vision, yet I fix my eyes forward and pedal harder. Why, why don't the neighbors complain? They can't, each one, have the slumber of saints. What twilight zone is this? Or is it that the surreal follows me around as an unshakable specter?

My nap is restless; I'm pitching and rolling on my rickety wrought-iron bed in a spastic dance, the dream I'd repressed for years returning. Shadowy figures in a circle are jabbing their fingers at me, exclaiming everything's my fault, while I sobbingly plead with them I'm not to blame.

It's not my fault mom left, or that dad broke; not my fault I couldn't piece them back together. What could I do at that age? When I snap out of the daymare, gasping for breath, my bedspread is sticky only with cool sweat. Lucky for me, it could've been worse. At least my pants are dry.

Near dusk, I stroll out my drab single-story house and past the tall tangled ferns tracing the lane, my head hanging between my shoulders and my hands fidgeting inside my pockets. I kick another loose stone in my tread.

They'll open a theme park in hell before Skunky mends his ways. Am I truly the problem here?

Near the opening, where the lane snakes into a quiet thoroughfare, an old uncle with sallow leathery skin sets in a squat, inspecting something on the asphalt. "Out to clear your head, son?" he asks in a small, unsteady voice.

Idle chatter is the last thing I wish to indulge, yet if I continue snubbing people from habit, I'm no better than

Skunky, am I? "I guess so," I mumble, trudging up to him.

He pokily gets to his feet, tosses up a large dirt-flecked chunk of chewing gum, and watches it mash against the road.

"Youngsters today," he says wistfully. "They ruin our sleep and destroy the planet. What to do?"

"What do you mean?" I ask, my eyes narrowing.

"Well, that kid, for example," he points to Skunky's princely two-story, "gets away with so much crap because his father loans cash to the neighboring drunks."

I nod along to his account, my brow knitting. No wonder the clamor didn't rouse those clowns, neither could Godzilla rampaging outside their door until its scaly claws were crushing their windpipes.

The old uncle shows a sad smile. "That's the way of our world, isn't it? Money solves everything." Asudden his face distorts from pain, and he dips forward, clutching his thigh.

I reach out a hand. "You okay?"

"Ha, yes. One of their bikes clipped me the other day. It was dark, and they didn't have their lights on."

He charily stretches his sore leg, grinning through the hurt, but I'm humorless, blowing out a long breath. Someday soon, that could be me. Tomorrow I must dig their graves.

Beyond the dim, twinkling streetlights, the night is sultry and windless, vacillating between eerie lulls and an artless concerto of canine howls and screechy cicadas. Thankfully, cooing nightjars will soon alight from their nests to snack on the demonic bugs and restore order to the universe.

In black from neck to toe, I sneak out my low gate, which I'm sure last wooed fresh paint in the colonial age, to spy left and right. Splendid, no busybodies promenading the street. I was smart to set my trap after dinnertime.

There he is, two homes up on the dirt mound between the driveways, the fleecy pooch resembling a giant cotton ball who's chomping on the strips of meat I earlier laced with sleeping pills.

My hands gleefully rub together while I smirk. Good, soon the pooch will go beddy-bye. Hey, why don't I try the same trick on his master? That might be my only means to repossess the frying pan.

I dart back into the house and return to the veranda with a stuffed duffel bag. A dark ski mask slips over my skull, and I pat the slim aerosol can in my pocket.

Satisfied with my prep, I again glance over the gate. Huh, where'd the dog disappear? No matter, I can't dawdle since Skunky and his crew will arrive in a few hours. I must suitably welcome them.

My gate squeakily parts, and upon slinging the duffel bag round my shoulder, I straightaway lower into a duckwalk and waddle out into the street.

There, and here, and there; I make a mental map of the darkest spots on the road. Then I draw a chalk out of my pocket, and scamper round the spots drawing small X's.

Next, short wooden planks emerge from the bag, painted black and crowned with sharp nails, which I meticulously arrange atop the X's and garnish them with glass shards. Hah, for an amateur vandal, you've outdone yourself, Holliday.

Soft growls and snapping poke my ears, and on a dime my heartbeat shifts up a gear. Uh-oh.

The pooch's inky eyes are gleaming, his bare canines glinting, and in a few steps he'll enter lunging distance.

Curses, how much sedative does it take to knock out this pygmy? My breath blows short and fast as I slink backward between the planks, my elbows held tight against my kidneys in a pugilistic pose. I hurl the chalk at his paws, but he doesn't flinch, and instead his growl deepens.

Goddammit, if this grinch hollers in his shrill, claxon-loud voice, the neighbors will think he's announcing a thief and there goes my plan. Argh, how is he still mobile?

My hand fumbles inside my pocket to retrieve the aerosol can, which I forthwith level at his mug. Any other time I'd admire his moxie, but tonight he mustn't ruin my revenge.

The pooch reacts by crouching forward, the slobber at the corners of his mouth thickening, and he's ready to bound at me.

Sorry, pal, you've forced my hand. A muted grunt escapes my throat when I squeeze on the spray nozzle for dear life, and straightaway a white cloud of chili pepper heat embraces the dog.

The pooch stops in his tracks from the threadlike mist, soon pawing his twitchy face over and over, before turning tail and sprinting upstreet, yelping.

My hand presses over my heart, my breath bursting in and out of my lungs. Please, Lord, let the comatose drunks lie undisturbed.

Ten seconds pass, and then a minute, but no porch lights flip on in the neighborhood. My palms slap my stiff legs into action, and I limp back inside the gate. Huff, huff, I'm far too nervy for a life of crime.

My room stays unlit when I flop into bed, reaching for the alarm clock on the scarred bedside table and clutching it over my breast. My pulse still outstrips the clock's ticking hand, and two glasses of water later, my thirst refuses to relent, as does the tingling in my limbs. Did I set the trap right? Did I forget something that'd point the cops to me?

CRASH.

I bolt upright, muzzy, the clockface pronto whacking my schnoz. And though my offended organ mightily throbs, I'm preoccupied with the tortured cries straining into the room. A skip later, I'm at the bedroom window, spying outside through the curtain gap.

Skunky and two of his pals are shimmying on their bikes, resembling a fat man's muffin top, and bearing straight for the steel dumpsters at the dead-end of the street.

SMASH. Smash. CLANG.

I pull back the oatmeal curtains, beaming. A half-dozen bikers in black-and-gray jumpsuits are writhing over the asphalt, holding one limb or another, whimpering.

Bruised sports bikes of various builds surround them, sprawled out on their bellies, their wheels aimlessly spinning. Past this breathtaking sight, a few busted taillights and cracked plates peek over the cavernous sewer beside the dumpsters.

I pull the curtains together, humming *Don't Fear the Reaper*, and fall into bed, lacing my fingers behind my head. Not long after, ambulance sirens echo in the distance, their pitch rising as they near the lane.

Ah, Holliday, tomorrow may again infuriate, but today at least, I'm the windshield and not the cicada.

It's a glorious morning awash in a blonde glow when I peel back the curtains to snoop round the street. City workers cleared the evidence without a second thought, and no cops are training a battering ram at my door. I don't say this enough, but God bless the dutiful drones.

I float out to the courtyard in my jammies, arching backward to stretch my arms wide. Coffee and work can wait, I must first act a good neighbor. Nothing beats a healthy dose of gloating to start the day right.

The short boundary wall of Skunky's house makes it easy to peek inside without appearing a stalker. He's on his sprawling patio, slouching on a rattan backyard swing, and brooding. Heavy bandages cover his arms and face, and his spiky hair hangs limply to his ears. Next to him, a prissy woman, his mother I assume, is shoving spoonfuls of gruel into his mouth.

Skunky catches my eye and sits up, glaring at me in an accusing manner. I politely wave at his mother and keep walking, but merely a few yards further, after which I tiptoe back to his wall. The woman soon rises with a brief admonishment and ambles into the mansion. Perfect.

My head shoots above the wall, and the second our eyes again meet, I flash him two dancing middle fingers, my face alight with a maniacal grin. Skunky tries to pull erect, glowering, but soon he groans and sags backward onto the cushions.

I palm my mouth, sniggering. The other foot, eh? What a magical place! Next, I should scour the black market for anthrax and mail a pinch to my boss. Yes, capital idea.

I'm swaggering toward my house when from behind a hand grabs my shoulder. Yaya. I'd find his stony countenance more unsettling if he hadn't reverted to his loony inside-out jacket and the mangy newsboy cap.

But the longer he frowns, the wrigglier get the worms

crawling up the pit of my stomach. Curses, don't tell me this was another test?

I scratch the back of my neck, simpering. "Hello there."

Yaya harrumphs and starts in a solemn tone, "Question time, son, so answer with care. Who did you avenge?"

Can he read thoughts too? He didn't catch the anthrax one, right? I glimpse my watch, swallowing. "I really should head to my audition."

"No need. You won't get the part."

My spine bows at his pronouncement. Why doesn't anyone believe in me? Am I a special breed of stupid to keep trying? "But shouldn't I give it a shot at least?"

Yaya snorts, his fingers snapping before my nose. "Again, who'd you avenge? Unless you don't care for Lady Luck's favor."

Such a noble word, avenge. I merely wanted release from my helplessness; to get back at someone, anyone. Skunky aroused my ire, true, but he wasn't my nemesis.

He was merely a pinata I could poke holes into without feeling guilty; a dartboard at which to focus my frustrations. "I did the right thing."

Yaya cackles, slapping his thigh. "I knew it. You're a terrible liar."

He fishes inside his jacket to recover a dog-eared notepad, and then produces a pen from under his cap, whereafter he licks his index finger a few times and starts scribbling.

Yaya is babbling under his breath as I bite at my bottom lip. What's going on here? Did I pass the test? "Um, the clue?"

He tears off a page with delicate flicks of the wrist and extends it toward me, his baffling Mona Lisa smile heightening my unease.

The lined paper shows a sketched turtle on one side, a plus and minus sign on the other. No dots or line. "What—"

The empty street beholds me without comment, and overhead the toylike finches deafeningly chirp.

I sink to the blacktop, my arms hugging my tucked knees, my forehead again and again rapping against them, and each time I groan louder. Curses, now what?

⌘

December Blucs

The year-end in Ipoh blows. Blows harder than a tubby red-faced trumpeter competing to win a lifetime's supply of chocolate drops by manually inflating an airship. Maybe it's me, but come December, I'm convinced every decent human in the food business skips town, leaving me alone to fend off the rascal restaurateurs and their family roaches.

There was a time I prided myself on my sensitive palate, firm in the belief this superpower promised me global fame as a genius sommelier. Bah, scratch that dream, though my tetchy gut isn't totally useless these days, for it has a supernatural knack for loudly grumbling near refried food that'll give me the runs.

The half-moon is tailing me while I slog uphill and against traffic. On either side of the four-lane road, colonial-style shop-houses flaunt their signature horseshoe arches, when round them the mechanical urban soundscape ebbs and flows. Frolickers in festive wear roam the streets in irregular clumps, chattering, unreasonably cheery.

Ack, how long have I been pedaling across town to land among the tourist traps? My relic-on-two-wheels parks next to a random curb, and drawing slow laborious breaths, I stow my arms atop the handlebar. Then my palm sweeps over the sweat misting on my forehead, an avalanche of swears crashing out from my parched lips.

Curses, I need grub pronto to stay conscious, but I cannot spend the night flossing my gums clean of roach feelers. Is proper hygiene asking too much of people who could otherwise poison you? Pity I didn't inherit my father's gift for digesting swill. Now, that man can lunch on sewer rat stew with a gusto equal to devouring mutton curry. Trust me, I did the switch twice to confirm it wasn't a fluke.

Leftward of me, a black tarpaulin banner sets on a T-stand, sets before a shop-house with a striking gold trim and slatted windows shimmering from the intense yellow streetlamps. In simple whiteface, the word amazon imprints on the banner, and nothing else. Humph, great marketing, morons.

My tummy again twinges from gastric stress, and I press on it, wincing. Holliday, give up your quest for the culinary Shangri-la. Even if one exists, its owners are likely vacationing at a seaside resort somewhere. Goddammit, you should've just swung by the delicatessen two stoplights earlier. What now?

I blunder off the bicycle, prop it against a lithe feathery tree that pops out the sidewalk, and drop onto the pavement, my head cradling in my arms. Should I thrust my palm out, pulling a miserable face, hoping a kindly passerby will donate cookies?

It's not long after that shades of music and merriment tickle my ears, drifting from behind the banner, from inside the tinted windows of the shop-house's ground floor.

Hmm, is that place an eatery? What's with their cloak-and-dagger look? No matter, Holliday, you're fresh out of blood sugar, so even if the mafia's picnicking in there, go grovel for their scraps, and if you must, dust off your old-man-on-deathbed routine. Heartless though the fiends may be, none can resist that pitiful face.

I nod to myself, resolute, the fleshy underside of my fist smacking into my open palm. My legs resurrect on the promise of sustenance, and I stride toward the shop-house, to its stout wooden door with the dungeon chic pull-ring.

Eh? Why won't it budge? I tug at the ring anew, my forearms cording, but with the same result. Then my knuckles rap on the stonelike wood twice and I wait. Inside, the festivities continue unabated, as if everyone's handily gone deaf.

Frowning, I shape my fist into a hammer and thump on the wood, awaiting a reaction, any meager recognition of my existence, but nothing. Goddammit.

Okay, it's possible I'm doing this wrong. I retreat two steps and outspread my hands, wiggling my fingers to mimic a dime-store magician, exclaiming "open sesame!"

Shortly, the music dies and the laughter fades. Oh, that worked? How absurd. But my relief instantly swaps for goose pimples when heavy footsteps approach the door. Uh-oh, if a hackneyed magical phrase alerted them to me, is a monster then headed my way?

The door rasps open, and promptly my toes furl up in my orthopedic flip-flops, my breath stalling from dread. Never in my life have I wished harder for disappointment.

A hulking beast emerges in the doorway, donning a baggy white apron under its poufed mullet, beholding me as if I stole its favorite mince pies. Man up, Holliday, act a coward on a full belly.

My shaky legs plant wide, and I puff out my chest and shrilly proclaim, "I want a drink."

At first the creature studies me unblinking, as if it's deciding the seasoning best suited to marinate me. Then it faces away and starts walking, its jalapeno-thick finger motioning me inside, to which I abide with furtive steps.

The spacious white-walled room reeks mightily of booze and crams with square cocktail tables and high steel chairs, and enough muscle to hurl a jetliner across the ocean. The patrons to a man sport dark athletic tops under their close-cropped hair, and shoestring pendants round their bullish necks.

My pulse is a greyhound on crack as their frosty stares pursue me over the bare tile floor, and toward the bar counter with the butcher-block top.

The beast circles round the counter and crosses its brawny arms. "What can I bring you?" it asks in a throaty voice.

Well, color me astonished. It's no wonder the pesky photographer at the company shoot last year obsessed over the right lighting. The stringy knot of incandescent ropes hanging overhead cast a soft marigold glow on the beast's features: handsomely masculine, akin to a construction worker pinup. Hell, at this rate, I too could model underwear as a side hustle.

Okay, Holliday, let's not push our luck and go with the safest bet. I plop on a barstool and offer the beast a pleasant smile. "A warm glass of milk, please, and perhaps some cookies on the side?"

I didn't think it possible, but Barkeep's deep-set eyes retreat further inside their sockets. "This is not your grandmother's kitchen the night before Christmas. Besides alcohol, we have water or juice. Take your pick."

Bah, still as personable as a serial killer. For an atomic second, I resolve to slam my fist against the bullnose countertop and demand better treatment, but Barkeep can perfectly snap my collar with a twist of the wrist, and so I feign meekness. "Orange juice then, but room temperature, please."

Soon music revives in the far corner, from the jukebox bizarrely fashioned as a sarcophagus, and the patrons are back to gabbing, no longer concerned with my person. Praise the Lord for my unimposing figure, or else I'd need a battery of bazookas to force my way out of here.

A tall glass slides to a stop beside my hand. Barkeep reaches out to mop up the spillover and starts toweling beer mugs, now and then glancing my way suspiciously. I timidly slurp on the juice, and straightaway my spirit soothes.

Ah, freshly squeezed! The glass empties in a flash from my gulps, and I set it on the countertop with a clunk. Barkeep's scowl is intact, but I care not. This was maybe worth risking my neck. Should I have another?

My face wears a goofy grin when I glance behind to the patrons. Should I try to make new friends? Not everyone in this joint should be a surly meathead. Why, the table nearest to me is full of laughs tonight.

"What's the difference between a girl and a gun?" one comedian quips. "The gun always has a point!" This punchline has them explode into mirthful braying, their fists again and again smacking the tabletop. And now that I'm mindful, other snippets of poor comedy waft round the joint, stabbing into my ears as a diamond point chisel.

Tsk-tsk. This must be one of those places that brutes with pea-sized packages frequent to mock women who won't date them. Doubtless that sharp musky scent tickling the back of my throat is pharmaceutical testosterone.

A laminate menu pokes my wrist. Barkeep signals to it, severe as ever, then spins round to the tall shelves to tidy up the liquor bottles thereon. I salivate when reviewing the fare. What photographic sorcery can turn everyday burgers and shakes into beauteous works of art? The orange juice rocked, so the food can't be abysmal, right?

I clasp my hands over the counter, my thumbs tapping together. Well, Holliday, the only question is one of survival. They're letting you be for now, but given Barkeep's demeanor, even a slight slipup could make you the proprietor of a lopped off head: your own. It'll go much easier if you can blend into the crowd. Hmm, a salty joke perchance?

I counter Barkeep's grim visage with a playful grin. "Women, I tell you, what a pain," I say, snickering. "If I had a dollar for every female driver I can't drive, I'd be a millionaire."

My snicker gains to flat-out giggling while Barkeep grunts derisively and shakes the head, but I know there's no curing this grouch. Can't be long now before the revelers erupt into belly laughs and someone buys me a drink.

"You want to repeat that?" a gruff voice says behind me.

They're built as battleships, the trio, and they radiate the warmth of angry rottweilers. Barkeep at once leaps over the countertop to join them.

My gut is a moth caught in a roaring tumble dryer. I lean away from them, my hands flying to my breast, my chin trembling. Curses, did I overdraw the act? "D-did I offend you?"

Their spokesperson has giant buttons for earlobes and the early days of a mustache. "You dare speak ill of women, you withered old fool?"

Their murderous glares have me speechless. This is insane. They started it, and mine was a good joke. Okay, okay, how do they defuse tense standoffs on TV? On those crime shows? Ah, right, act assertive but affable.

I sit upright, my breath rushing. "What's the problem? I'm sure you fine gentlemen have a funny bone or two," I say, forcing a wink.

The bar posthaste hushes, besides chairs scraping over the tiles, the pointed stares of their occupants flushing me the shade of eggplants. Argh, useless busybodies, the group of them.

The trio are cracking their knuckles, and Buttons's forearms are a spiderweb of veins straining against skin. "What's this gentlemen crap, huh?"

Curses, why did the bar outstretch into a soccer field, and why does it spin madly? And why is the Moby Dick of doors on a different planet? Ack, pull yourself together, Holliday. Maybe they're too dimwitted to grasp your humor. Focus, focus. What to say so you'll walk out alive? How do those cocky frauds handle such in the movies?

My hands raise in surrender. "Fine, fine. Don't go all womanly on me," I suggest, simpering.

No sooner do I say so that their collective groan rings through the room.

"We are women, dumbass," Buttons screeches.

My arms lower to my lap while I behold them with a simian deadpan. "Right, and I'm Mata Hari."

They respond with death stares, muttering among themselves. My neck cranes forward to eavesdrop, but I'm unable to decipher their intent, since the god-awful ringing in my ears won't subside. Women, they say. What stupidity. Anyone can see...

I do a double-take and my ears turn hot, impossibly hot, as though they're donuts dunking in a steaming mug of acid. Those chiseled pecs, they're too perky. And the name, the bar's name. Holliday, you effing idiot.

"Hello," I say, fiddling with my shirtsleeve. "How about I kiss your magnificent boots and we call it quits?"

They ignore my plea, now huddling with their backs to me, feverishly whispering and jabbing their fingers. The patrons follow their lead, leaning toward one another while glimpsing me sidelong, their expressions screaming disgust.

The searing heat spreads to my cheeks, and my chin droops to my chest. I'd have them execute me on the spot, if I wasn't such a shameless coward.

Meanwhile, the ticktock of the kitschy oversized wall clock grows deafening, as if alerting me my end is nigh. Roach-fried rice doesn't sound so dreadful anymore. After tonight, I may not have a gut to guard against vermin.

A sudden flick to the nose shatters my funereal trance. Buttons is inches from me, swimming in the stench of sour bananas. Her thin almond eyes are stony and her lopsided lips curl at the corners. "Drink or death. What'll it be?"

My Adam's apple is working overtime to swallow her threat. Drink? As in liquor? Unacceptable. The last time I partook in a bender, a decade ago no less, I rang up the entire family to express my profound love. I cannot, cannot relive that horror.

My disquiet casts itself into a pout. "I don't get it. Why are you treating me like pond scum? That's just unfair."

"No, no, we're sick of you men putting women down to satisfy your egos," Buttons says, stepping away, her finger waggling back and forth. "You'll drink till we drop or end up a bloody pulp. Your choice."

My legs fervently twitch from the want to stay stuck to the rest of me. Time for one last gamble, Holliday. How did it go again, your terminal old man routine?

Tuck in your elbows at the chest, and contort your fingers into gnarly claws, check. Next, get your knees hitching as though you're stuck in a subzero snowstorm, check. Then suck in your cheeks to mimic day-old roadkill, check.

And for the finishing touch: "I have a medical condition," I say in a world-weary croak.

Not a smidgen of empathy flashes across their faces. "If you don't comply, you'll wish you did," Barkeep says, checking her nails.

The room now gyres without form; first it swells as a parachute, then flattens into a pancake. My arms are leaden at my sides, popping sounds aimlessly escaping my mouth.

Figures, Holliday. Who else could the cosmic joker pick for such wicked comedy? A middle-aged man walks into a female muscle bar and mistakes them for men. Ba-dum-tss. This'll make the Weekly Loser's highlights reel every year.

I mumble my assent, and right away the villains hurrah, and glasses clink round the bar. Buttons and Barkeep scamper to behind the counter, to its lightless corner, soon returning with an octagonal table which they unfold while smirking at me.

My middle finger fiddles in response, but the worry of them uniting me with its aluminum frame simmers my boil.

Buttons is stocking the table with assorted libations while Barkeep joyously claps and skips in her spot. "Yay, we should do dares," she says.

Half-forgotten prayers rise to my quivering lips. Somebody, anybody, save me. I fear dares with these barbarians could mean a life sentence without parole.

Wow, how'd they even let me into this place? The ornate theater has a glassy cupolated roof and decks with brilliant rock-crystal chandeliers, while before me on the epic red-carpet stage sets a splendorous see-through lectern holding pages of my chicken scratch.

Yonder, a rapt audience in monkey suits and cocktail dresses awaits my life-changing speech. Oh, there's Dorothy and Toto too, sitting ten rows back and waving at me.

Hah, I'm their alpha and omega, and now I must dazzle them. Shoulders back, I check the ears of my bow tie and button up my bespoke tuxedo jacket. Well, I was born for this.

"Hello," I declare, and promptly a mutant housefly the mass of a marble whizzes past my teeth and lights a cigar in my lungs. I double over, gripping my neck, gagging from the sensation of sucking in oxygen through a pinhole.

Before long, invisible hands lock round my waist, and inward and upward they thrust, jerking me round as a rag doll before I black out on stage.

Thirsty, so thirsty. Curses, who set the air-con to arctic? There's a dull thumping in my head, as though a rubber hammer unceasingly beats against my crown. Then someone turns up the soundtrack to my misery: shuffling feet, and beeping cellphones, and strangers murmuring.

My fingers grope over the cool tiles. Goddammit. I force open a logy eye to sight the familiar ceiling, and then my hand pats over my breast and I choke on a sob. No tuxedo. I'm back in the nightmare called reality.

My achy leg stretches, and pronto my toes slam against metal, upon which I will myself upright, my eyes squinching from pain and the need to steady my vision.

A standard-issue office desk flanks the near wall, and behind it, someone clutches a newspaper to their face. And beside the stout door now seats a woman in navy-blue scrubs, attending to a queue of whey-faced persons from behind her desk. Off and on, they're stealing glances at me and whispering to one another.

A clinic? Given the bare fixtures, a government one. What the hell happened here?

I growl under my breath. Satan has nothing on those birdbrains. Screw access, how did they dismantle the bar overnight? Do they repeat this every evening? What criminal geniuses. Either way, I must scram before a cop decides he needs cough syrup.

"Excuse me," I croak at the person reading the news. "Can I get a glass of water?"

A pair of fiery eyes peek over the brim, and then the paper lowers and I behold a sinister grin. "You're alive? Good, the police are on their way."

A horror-stricken squeal leaves my mouth, and my palms paddle me away from the desk. Buttons. No effing way. She dons the same scrubs, and with sorcery unknown, she's grown silken locks that now brush her shoulders.

"You should prepare yourself for a public lynching," Buttons says in a smug tone, doubling the newspaper and holding it in my direction.

A sting fires through my chest as a falling star zipping through space. I made the top of the metro page, but for the wrongest reason. It's me, freely pissing on the mural likeness of a local icon, sticking my tongue out and flashing the devil's horns.

I sense my heart shrinking smaller and smaller from dread. Since breakfast, I've without question outdone Hitler in the number of people that want me dead. They will hang me from a flagpole by my nuts and grind my corpse into dog chow.

Buttons slaps the paper on the desk, then leans back in her swivel chair, tying her fingers behind her head. "Ha-ha, cellphone cameras, how did we ever make do without them?"

Argh, where's a syringe when you need one to gouge out her eyes? I rise into a crouch, glowering at her. "Why'd you do this to me?"

She shrugs, doing a sturgeon face. "What else is the holiday season for, if not pranks?"

"How about prayer, you gorilla?" I snap.

Buttons's palm faces outward to signal our exchange is over, and she goes back to perusing the paper. "Stop making a fuss. They're other sick people here," she says with a raffish smile.

My teeth grind to dust as I imagine countless gruesome scenarios of her decapitation. Curses, that photo makes it hard to frame her, meaning the only way to save my family jewels is by acting the sorry victim of their obscene prank.

But first, I need to flee.

I raise my hand above and away from my face, my eyes shutting tight and my lips drawing taut. This will mother-loving hurt.

SMACK.

My hand meets my cheek in a thunderclap, and I fling myself to the floor. Buttons startles for a beat, pushing back her chair and gaping at me.

My chest hits the floor when I'm reaching out an arm toward the queue. "Help, she's trying to kill me," I holler, crawling toward the door.

A few patients are craning their necks, squinting, trading confused looks. Then Buttons's chair bangs against the wall and I'm bellying faster over the tiles, curbing the instinct to look back.

Her footsteps stamp with a ferocity that rattles my ribcage, my pulse pounding in my throat. Moment of truth, Holliday. If she doesn't care for her reputation, you're dead. Ditto, if she convinces them you're a crazed druggie.

Fright propels me into a butterfly stroke across the floor, but Buttons forthwith grips my ankles and effortlessly drags me back as though I'm a sack of potatoes.

Then she flips me onto my spine, her face twisted into a hobgoblin's, her hamlike fist flirting with the tip of my nose.

"The morgue van at the back," she hisses, and my nostrils again melt from the stench of rotting bananas. "Leave."

I can't help but respect the departed, for the way they treat us is a travesty. Not only do they strip our dignity to a side-less toga inside full-body plastic, the morgue hires drivers who're hell-for-leather loonies.

Once more the van swerves pell-mell, and sliding up the steel gurney, my heels smack against the wiry mesh separating my white-hot fists from the moron impersonating a professional. Bah, you just wait, I'll drive you to the graveyard myself.

As for the gorilla, if she forgets to mail my stuff home, I'll rig my bicycle with explosives and park it next to her desk. If nothing else, that'll nuke her high horse and the hairpiece on her swollen head.

The van brakes asudden, bucking as an irate mule, and my bare toes twist against the grill. I utter a pained cuss while the driver's side door clicks open and shuts. Ack, where's the wastrel headed? Are we across state lines yet?

My fingers claw through the body bag zipper, and I squiggle upright on the gurney to spy through the windows. A roadside restaurant? Oh, Malaysians.

My tummy is grumbling now, but I have no clothes. Did I eat last night? No, no, don't bend your brain, Holliday, no piecing that puzzle. Who knows what other hell they put you through for their amusement? Well, this way I'm making a fashion statement, right? And I can't sink any lower than playacting a corpse.

My hand depresses the chunky double-door handle, and I steal out the van onto the toasty asphalt. Splendid, no busybodies palming their hearts, or grim cops fumbling for their radios. For a change, the heavens aren't actively plotting my disgrace.

The late morning sun tingles my skin and the toga lets a gentle breeze up my privates. My fingers twine behind my neck, and I contentedly sigh. Pants are so overrated.

I waddle into the diner to find the pimpled stocky van driver in white togs gawking at me, now nibbling on his soggy flatbread at glacial speed. I throw him a curt wave and mosey along to an empty table where a piercing whistle carries from my lips.

"One of everything, bro," I say when the spooked server slinks up to me.

He stares at me endlessly and without comment. Fair enough, to him I must appear an asylum escapee. "Okay, okay, fried rice then."

The next thing I know, a plain peanut-brown clipboard flies before my face. The van driver is standing beside me, his finger drumming its edge. "Please confirm you're alive."

My downturned mouth lets out a snort when I slide out the stringed pen to sign his wordy form. "Humph. You don't have to mourn the fact."

I shove the clipboard back at the driver, and without fanfare he tears off a piece and deposits it on the table. "Your receipt. Hope you're keeping the others safe," he says dully and ambles away.

It's a ringlike scrap with jagged edges. I straighten in the chair, licking my lips. Naturally, both driver and van have vanished without a trace.

Curses, how many minions does Yaya have? And what witch's portal allows them to jump through time and place as they please?

There's a smiley drawn on one side, but no dots or lines anywhere. I touch my forehead, releasing a noisy breath. Is this good? What's the score, goddammit? Am I winning or losing? Bah, I ought to flog the geezer with a nail bat.

The piquant aroma of fried rice sends my appetite into overdrive and drool builds in the corner of my mouth.

"Anything else, boss?" the server drawls.

I peer at him seriously, wiping my mouth clean of the spittle. "Yes. When can I wash the dishes?"

⌘

The Termite Whisperer

The bruises on my arms and cheeks endorse the fact a wretched man takes good news as he does a punch in the kisser: reeling and dumbstruck. To be fair, it's a miracle my flesh only contused from pinching myself over and over, and didn't instead shed to the floor as knotty clumps.

Though we're past lunchtime, the drafty agency cafeteria still crowds with my colleagues, many as me donning neon vests, while the rest sport unicolor clip-on ties over chintzy half-sleeved shirts. What unites them is their bored looks, and the way they loll over the laminate long benches to my rear. They're picking their noses, and they're burping, and yet they're staying back since each is a dependable serf.

Well, well, Holliday, what a shocker. First, that stingy bloodsucker of a boss halves your work hours to make you consider quitting, but now he wants to celebrate your donkey's years at the agency? With a cash bonus, no less? Hah, is he dying? His ordinarily boyish complexion today carries a jaundiced look, but more to the point, the Satan I know is incapable of acting decent without a catch.

Still, you never thought you'd live to see this day, eh? For sure dad never did, adamant I'd spend the rest of my life living paycheck to paycheck, a conviction he took great pains to echo through my teens. Hell, my moving out the house stunned him speechless.

In the early days, dad himself shared he'd sometimes barge into my former room, convinced he'd find me hiding in the cupboard, freeloading on his favorite cookies. I should pass him the good news the instant the ceremony ends, and hopefully he'll save face by allowing himself a massive stroke.

Boss is at the head of the cafeteria, standing atop a creaky, makeshift stage in his denim-blue safari suit, conferring in hushed tones with an oily lackey from the mayor's office. Minion, said lackey, clutches a leathery folder to the front of his khaki notch-lapelled jacket, bearing the permanent false smile of a trainee politician.

Before long, Minion alone drifts to the stage's lip, coughing into his fist to rouse the snoozers. "This afternoon, we celebrate the service of a public safety veteran who's saved many a child and drunk from crushing into pavement pizza. Our senior crossing guard, Mr. Holliday!"

The serfs break into tepid claps as I swoop up the stage, flaunting a mile-wide grin. My hand outstretches to meet Minion's in a swift pump, and I promptly snatch the folder. Then I straighten toward the photographer and flip open its cover, awaiting his camera's telltale clicks.

Hey, what's the damn holdup, son? How hard is it to press a big button next to your nose? But he's lowering the camera, gaping at my navel, and altogether the audience gasps. Huh? Is my fly open? They can't know I'm wearing the same drawers two days in a row.

It takes but a twinkle for my blood pressure to shoot to the stratosphere, my groan deepening to a growl. Why, effing why?

My hard-won certificate is missing chunks in the shape of small figure eights, as though a tiny lawnmower flew helter-skelter on the card stock. My breath blows sharp and shaky, a bestial rage seizing every fiber of my being.

It takes every ounce of my willpower to not deck Minion when he leans in with a concerned look, his hand placing on my shoulder, his jaw sounding speech I can't hear. My tunnel-vision only knows the figure behind him, the sole object of my murderous thoughts.

Boss. He's responsible, I just know it. Bah, the fiend is busy on his cellphone after wrecking my big day. Don't think I won't disembowel you with the folder, you little… why's he shuddering?

Boss meets my glare, bug-eyed, his plump wrist mopping the pellets of sweat on his forehead. "T-termites."

My superior has a gift for stealing the simple joys of life. Every time I've run into him this year, the memory of secretly scrawling fangs and horns on his company yearbook photo made me snicker to myself, but no more.

Since earlier this morning, he's been silently staring into space while biting on his bottom lip; channeling his inner Little Bo-Peep, who's lost her sheep and her sanity.

Boss's twin-pedestal desk is unmistakably chaotic, and a fusty odor hangs over his smart office as if someone dusted the furniture with moldy bread. Through my time at the firm, I've never enlisted for extracurricular messes, but those bugs ruined my moment of glory and so I must squish them. And I want the damn bonus he owes me.

"Why him?" I finally ask.

He startles at my voice. "He's the best there is."

"And where is that? The loony bin?"

"You don't understand, son," Boss says, clawing at his double chin. "The payroll records, the invoices, they're all gone. We're under attack by a sinister force of nature."

He returns to his trance, his restless fingertips drumming the desk, while I slouch in my chair, my lips clamping together in annoyance. Bah, with so grave a threat, why ask a lunatic to head the cavalry?

The last I saw thirty minutes ago, his so-called exterminator was bustling round the office floor knocking on walls and cupping his ears against them, perchance expecting the bugs to answer with how-do-you-dos and an invitation to tea.

The way I understand it, on planet Earth, a pest handler shows up and sometime later strolls out with a cageful of critters sans fuss or fanfare. But here, in the alternate universe of stupid, Boss hired a hoary termite whisperer who's twisted a simple task into the national dog and pony show.

The door flings open, and voilà, the genius himself, Whispy, saunters inside and plops into the chair beside mine. His pasty, bony face strikes me as solemn, and his blinding tie-dyed overalls carry fresh dirt stains. Boss tips forward over the desk, peering at him in the manner of a lost puppy.

Whispy crosses his legs and wriggles his turquoise toenails.

"You were right to call me, bro. I fear the problem is graver than a simple trap-and-toss routine," he says, wheezing as a punctured accordion.

Boss obediently nods, and a sudden disquiet grips my nerves. Curses, the geezer is setting him up to charge extra. These scammers never miss a trick, do they? Now my cheapskate superior has the perfect excuse to delay my cash prize, if not shelve it completely.

"Why? The termites going on a hunger strike?" I ask Whispy, frowning.

He tut-tuts at me, resembling a pompous priest. "No, no, these are no mere insects. They're fragments of restless souls, the souls of people wronged by this agency."

Not a sliver of surprise flashes over Boss's face. "Okay, when can you rid us of these pests?"

I sit upright, my jaw slackening. "You're not serious."

Whispy's stroking his scruffy ducktail beard. "I can have them leave, bro, but that requires ancient voodoo. That said, if you're willing to fork out the cash, I guarantee they won't gnaw on your bones next."

Ba-dum-tss! As I suspected. Goddammit, why doesn't my foresight ever favor me? "You believe his ridiculous campfire story?" I ask, incredulous.

Boss pays me no mind, now pressing his fingertips together on the desktop while eyeing Whispy with a determined expression. "Deal. Do what you must."

Whispy wears a toothy grin when reaching out his hand. "Prepare the cash, and remember, I get rid of all pests, period."

A weary sigh escapes me, my head lightly shaking in disbelief. Where's God when you need two precise thunderbolts?

This is insane, so insane I could soil my pants. I'm perching atop the chair, the fluffy broom at my waist quivering without pause, my nose over and over twitching from the smoggy incense flooding the office. Now and then I shift from one foot to the other, to prevent my legs from turning to stone, but I dare not ground them.

An hour ago, when Whispy instructed us to take cover, I announced I'd head to my crosswalk, but that plan went bust the moment Boss, goddam him, pithily reminded me my bonus was at stake. So here I am, witnessing the graybeard's madcap charade instead of planning my splurge. Argh, my talent for finding myself at the wrong place at the worst time keeps sharpening.

Since the ritual began, Boss hasn't uttered a peep, sitting crossed-legged and hunched forward atop his desk, his unblinking eyes fixed on the exterminator. Whispy, meanwhile, sets his haunches in the middle of the room, donning a skullcap with two taut feelers.

A pluming incense bowl places beside him on the tweedy wall-to-wall carpet, and round him he's sprinkling a white powder he pinched from his pocket. Normally I'd assume it was insect repellent, but knowing him it's something far more ruinous.

Then the fruitcake concludes he hasn't appalled us enough, and starts hopping inside his circle, cooing and cackling in every direction, his neck jabbing back and forth resembling a mad rooster. And with each pushed breath his spit sprays far and wide, and without warning, one such coo thickens into a loogie that cannons into my neck.

I wipe the slime off with my wrist, staring daggers at him, but Whispy's moved on to the encore: a lively Russian squat dance while he's yodeling in the key of a tone-deaf hippo. Bah, if they'd never outlawed mob executions in Malaysia, he'd be the perfect candidate to break in a new guillotine.

His vexing farce ends on a dime when he stretches out on his tummy to put his ear against the rug, his shrewd eyes alive with excitement. "They're coming."

A whimper rises to my throat. Coming? Did they arrange for their own funeral? I get to my feet, holding out the broom as a saber, my fingers again and again flexing round its handle. "Who's coming, you crackpot?"

A dry rattle. It swells in the room, and then the infernal critters burst into view. Legions of black, red and brown termites crawl out of the woodwork, out the walls, and stunningly, by gnawing through the carpet.

My palm at once flies to my heart, which threatens to burst through my chest. Boss, too, cowers at their sight, his arms wrapping round his belly, his countenance terror-stricken. I labor to suck in air, beseeching God over and over to save me, promising I'll never again spit in Boss's takeaway.

The termites congregate midway between us and Whispy, their feelers wiggling with greater intensity, and then they're piling atop one another to build an obelisk the height of a footstool. Unperturbed, the old-timer is flapping his arms as a giant bird, in the same breath starting an off-key chant comparable to a mule singing the opera.

Though I cover my ears, grimacing, the termites respond to his ruckus with striking obedience, right away breaking into neat lines and trooping toward him in lockstep.

Then Boss screams, and I unwittingly become the chorus. His face waxen, his tremulous finger is pointing to the carpet, to the band of rogue termites who broke away from the core and are scuttling toward us, their feelers writhing violently. This time we shriek together as hysterical toddlers.

Whispy ceases his chanting to snicker at our terror, soon after slotting his pinkie tips between his lips to sound a piping whistle. The villainous hexapods freeze in their tracks pronto, at which point he whistles anew and they hotfoot it back to the others.

Once the termites gather round him, Whispy sweeps away the powder with his heel, grabs the incense bowl, and darts to the doorway. There, he flashes us a victory sign, "Be right back after saving their souls." The coos and cackles revive on his lips as he shepherds out the evil empire.

Boss straightens on the desk, tugging at his sweat-soaked collar, coolly nodding at me. "And that, Holliday, is how you solve problems."

ACHOO. Huff, huff, huff. In this latest episode of Holliday's woe-is-me truths, I've realized few things in life tax you more than sneezing and sticking your scalded tongue out in one breath. Yay for me.

Damn the flu, damn this diner, damn my steaming gingerroot-and-honey tea, and damn the floppy-hatted moron seated one row up who pogos every few seconds to ruin my TV viewing.

Sniveling, I pull my tumbledown hoodie tighter around me, then reach for the tacky plastic box on my table to swipe a fistful of tissues. I freely blow my nose out of my skull, indifferent to the repulsed looks that straightaway fix on me.

The only upside of my illness is I haven't seen Boss or Whispy for days. Bah, I'm lucky I'm still breathing. It's no minor miracle my delicate schnoz weathered those caustic fumes posing as incense without fleeing my face. That stupid geezer, hope the critters unionize someday and entomb him underground.

Uh-uh, says the bothersome little man inside my head. Wrong, Holliday, wrong. This is Boss's fault, the tightfisted toad. He's the one those restless souls want, so why must we suffer? God knows when we'll get that bonus, if ever. Don't delay the inevitable. Gas prices are still cheap, so let's stock up and find…

Hey, isn't that the work building? The news on TV has switched to clamorous scenes of protest in the parking lot, where a gang of crossing guards are waving placards in the air, shouting, "Down with the demon."

I cock forward in my slablike seat, clasping the tea mug for another swig, my eyes tightening. This is new. I'm away a few days and the entire place goes to hell?

The camera now pans to a glassy-eyed rookie who's mumbling into a microphone, "We've had enough. The monster has harassed us enough. Down with the monster." Then he defiantly shoots up his knuckled fist and spits to the side.

I swallow my lips while scratching my scalp. This is so unfair. How could they forget me? If they were planning a coup, was I not the perfect bitter melon to plant in the vanguard?

The broadcast cuts to the top step of the building's brief perron, whereon a suited man clutching a bullhorn is addressing the crowd. Minion? What's he doing there?

"…I promise you change starts today. You have opened our eyes to this demon in the heart of our beloved city," he says, raising a dramatic hand to the heavens.

"Fear not, heads will roll and justice will prevail…"

What effing justice and what effing demon? I slip my phone out from under the hoodie and dial Boss's number, but every time the call rings out and goes to voice-mail. Why? Did he wimp out on spotting the mob? That's very unlike him, instead I thought he'd have a sniper on the roof to scare them away.

"…now let me introduce the upstanding gentleman who helped expose this evil," Minion says, gesturing to someone out of frame.

My cellphone meets the tabletop with a clatter, shock whacking me in the solar plexus as a heavyweight boxer's straight. No, no way. The so-called gentleman is Whispy, now striding center-stage in inky aviators and brightly hailing the crowd.

On a sudden the camera zooms into his mug, and he snaps off his shades to wink at me with a roguish grin. What the hell? My hands fussily scrub over my face.

Curses, has my flu advanced to delirium? But when I peek through my fingers, the screen is back to a wide-angle view, and not a soul round me wears a hint of surprise.

The nuisance sporting the floppy hat swings round to me, setting his arm against the top rail of his chair. "Well, isn't that something," he says, wryly smiling.

"Boss," I exclaim.

Gaunt and stubbly, he resembles laundry left inside a washing machine over the weekend and freshened with moonshine.

Boss disregards my slack-jawed stare and continues wistfully, "The takeaway, young grasshopper is to never provoke a man who can talk to termites, or he'll turn you into vermin." He glances to Minion raving on TV. "And never, ever consort with the government."

Wow, he stiffed Whispy after witnessing his spooky mojo? What an idiot. "You didn't pay him? Have you gone insane?"

Boss lets out a mirthless laugh and it trails. "Scruples don't make money now, do they? Anyway, it was about time the sins of the ancestors crashed on this son."

His chin dips toward the floor dispiritedly, his features darkening. I squirm in my seat, flipping open my phone, pretending to check for messages.

The pesky voice resurfaces to scold me. Holliday, Holliday, don't pity the tyrant. He's making excuses to not pay us our due. Call the agency right now and alert them to his presence. He deserves to rot in jail; you know that, and they'll honor us as heroes. Isn't that what we want?

My lungs empty in a long, muted sigh. Yes, but if I pour fuel on his suffering, how am I any different from my father? Or those aunts and uncles who always heckled me for dreaming big? "You want something to drink?" I ask Boss, forcing a grin. "It can't be all that bad."

Boss lifts his head and casts me a slight, fleeting smile. Then he rises and shuffles past me without a word. I avoid his gaze and return to the TV, jiggling the jammed zipper of my hoodie. Oh well, I tried. The hurt of an outcast won't disappear overnight, or ever, to be honest.

Shortly, a tubby palm slaps on the table, and I jerk backward, alarmed. Boss draws away his hand, uncovering a paper scrap beside my mug. "You pass, it seems."

My neck bends forward, and I rapidly blink. The paper carries two dots and a line, but today they're running the other way. Hang on, is this the last task? Have I succeeded or failed the quest? Argh, I've never known, thanks to that brain-dead dolt, Yaya.

I meet Boss's somber stare. "W-where did you get this?"

"The geezer ordered me to give it to you," he says, fidgeting with the brim of his hat. "That's why the mob hasn't lynched me yet."

"Whispy?" I croak.

Boss's head tilts to one side, his nose wrinkling. "Funny. Why can't I recall?"

That instant his eyes glaze over and they roll back into his head, his pudgy frame spasming as though an icy specter seizes him. I'm pulling erect, asking Boss if he's okay, but he can't, or won't, hear me while he's dashing for the exit.

Whispy's still on TV, the bullhorn against his mouth, his hands gesturing wildly as he paces before the spellbound protesters. The paper sticks between my thumb and forefinger, and I absently caress its surface, my breath cinching from a profound poverty of hope.

Now what, Holliday? Do I even have a job anymore? Bah, why has only misfortune stalked me since I began the quest?

My cellphone is bucking on the tabletop, making the mug clink and the flatware rattle. Hmm, why's the agency calling?

The line is noisy with strident slogans, the specifics of which elude me. "Mr. Holliday? How would you like a promotion?" a frantic male voice asks.

Another divine comedy? Well played, God. Your timing is, as always, apocalyptic. "Look here," I snap. "Is this another one of your harebrained schemes to dump company umbrellas? I already own a small mountain under my bed."

"No, no, this is for real. Unless you're unsure after the news story?"

The gloom holding me hostage fades away forthwith, and instead a tiny sun fires up in my soul. For real? Am I, am I winning? This can't be a trick, right? Not even Yaya can be that cruel. "N-not for a second. I'm in."

"Good, good. Now remember, and this is very important, if anyone asks, you never saw Boss."

Huh? How in blazes does he know? Who are these people? I noisily free my throat of nerves. "Who?"

⌘

— Week Seven —

Tambun Jun and the Terrors

Should I ask them to bury me here; under these sooty tiles, a stack of forks, spoons, and cracked ceramic teacups for my tombstone? Why am I drawn to this infernal greasy spoon every time I'm bleak and cheerless? Is it because my house walls whisper to me when it's quiet? Tell me I'm worthless scum, that I should buy rat poison and end my suffering?

Bah, stupid walls. No way I'm committing myself to the asylum until they add Western movie channels to their lounge TV. Not going to happen.

At the diner it's the same every day: a rinse-and-repeat cycle of regulars absently picking at their food, their jaded, glassy-eyed demeanors unchanging, their dull prattle unceasing. I often yearn for their insouciance toward life, and though I've tried, such a godsend is beyond me. If I could only convince myself to impersonate a pebble, I'd surely be happier.

I'm thumbing through a small pile of newspapers, skimming over their classifieds while sipping on weak black tea and pulling back cusses. Doubtless I'd concoct a more satisfying brew if I mixed mud to boiling water, and I'd likely steal tastier food from rats scavenging a dumpster.

And I'd never need allergy medicine if not for the fiery spices befogging the air, forever holding my nostrils hostage on the precipice of a fatal sneeze. Since I've never wished for my gray matter to spray out as snotty chunks, why, oh why, do I return?

Ack, has the diner someway bewitched me? Is it alive, a supernatural octopus born of a tear in time and space? Are its fanged tentacles in disguise as slowpoke servers and a cashier who sucks on lemons for breakfast?

For sustenance, does it pierce my soul to feast on my sorrows and those of the zombies round me? Small wonder it won't let me go, for I am a most valuable asset. There's scarcely a soul alive who'd best my natural talent for unearthing misery. Sigh, say it ain't so, Holliday, say it ain't so.

I brusquely fold the newspaper, toss it on the table, and take my head in my hands. Why does this happen to me? Finally, I get a promotion, and pronto the stooges in city hall shutter the agency for an audit. Argh, why is that band of jokers forever late to the punch? They never forget to eat, do they? Sigh, no sign of Yaya or Lady Luck. Why tell me to keep those scraps of paper? What will become of me?

It won't be long before my landlord is at it again, pestering me for rent, dusting off his pompous spiel on my duties as a tenant. Before, I groveled for an extension on account of my slashed work hours, but what excuse do I peddle now? Is it too late to entreat my disowned uncles to teach me the drug trade? Scruples are for fools, and I'm living proof. Pathetic.

"Hello, bro," a bright voice says above me. "Happy birthday, right?"

That bold hook nose and those beady eyes. Great, just the person to hasten my suicidal rampage. I should rearrange Hooky's features for sending me into the pint-size demon's lair, maybe rip off his beak and resew it to his rump, but as I am, my arms can't duel a gnat, much less dent his lardy flesh.

He, the world champion of mannerless cretins, plonks into the chair opposite mine sans my invitation. Then he locks his fingers together and flexes out his arms, allowing me a sad smile. "I hear they're investigating the agency."

Hooky's knowledge doesn't surprise. Rotten news travels lightning fast in the backwaters, and no matter where, busybodies have their own wire service. I fake a yawn, outspreading a newspaper before my face in the dim hope he'll leave. "Yea."

His finger insistently pokes at the fold as if he were a bored three-year-old. "Disgraceful, bro, disgraceful. So, what're your plans?"

Quick breaths draw through my clenched teeth as I contain the urge to double the newspaper into a baton and chase him from the diner. "Think I'll join the family trade." If the uncles aren't together on death row, that is.

He sniggers half a second longer than is socially acceptable. "I can guess the trade."

The vein in my temple fiercely twitches. Can't this idiot read the mood? I smack the broadsheet against the tabletop and throw him the stink eye. "You're here to gloat, is it?"

Hooky startles, his lips forming an O, his hands waving in apology. "No, no. I have a business proposition for you."

I sound a loud grunt, leaning back in my chair and crossing my arms. "Which is? Wrestling tigers this time, eh?"

He voices a nervous laugh akin to a whining car engine, his eyes darting round the diner, his hand dragging over his glistening shaved dome. "How about earning some money and my eternal gratitude?"

Wow, where does his kind find the cheek? "No thanks. After last time, I'd rather take my chances with the big cats. At least I know their intentions."

Hooky solemnly bows his head, his palms clamping together at his heart in a praying pose. "Pinkie swear, my offer is genuine. I really thought it was a regular meeting."

Well, isn't this a wondrous day? I never imagined he could count to twenty in one go, much less display a capacity for contrition. No time to nitpick, Holliday. You need money, and thus his offer must be a sign from the heavens. Here you remembered your uncles, and voila, a man who looks the part of a career pusher shows.

"Continue," I say, deadpan.

Hooky raises his chin, his mouth framing a simper. "Thing is, I promised to take my kids to the theme park, but the company won't allow time off unless I find a replacement. And the young ones insist we go today."

Please don't tell me…"And?"

He's twirling his thumbs one over the other, his simper now stretching to bare his ivories. "Can you replace me for today? I know it's sudden, but I can't trust anyone else. And it pays well, too."

A groan rings in my brain. Sigh, so much for overnight riches. Why can't the haves trust in me as the plebs do?

"How good?"

"Three hundred dollars. Good, right?"

I pull upright on my seat. "For a day's work?"

Hooky nods and straightaway the invisible boulder crushing my rib cage lifts. Hey, that's enough to ride this month out without stealing lunch from schoolkids.

"Yes, that'll do, I guess."

"Wonderful," he says, rubbing his hands together. Then he unslings the bloated satchel off his shoulder and sets it on the tabletop. "All yours. Make sure you deliver these today," he says, patting the satchel's coarse canvas body.

I hesitate while he stares at me keenly, for the bloody obvious just hit me with a brick's force. Doesn't he use a moped to drive round town? Curses. The last time I took dad's scooter for repairs, I nearly crashed into a cop, who thereupon chased me up the road until I rammed into a traffic pole.

I claw at my cheek, swallowing hard. "Um, I haven't used a moped in years."

Hooky chuckles at my concern, dismissing it with a flap of his wrist. "You own a bicycle, right? No worries. Only, don't brake too hard or you'll fly off to Africa, and don't curve too fast or it'll fall apart, ha-ha."

The corners of my mouth wrinkle while I frown at him. Everything's a joke to these birdbrains until tragedy befalls them, and then it's the government's fault. Well, nothing for it, I'll recite the half-prayers I remember and drive at a snail's pace.

"Your rust bucket better not flame up today," I say, unzipping the satchel.

He pretends not to hear me, instead starting into a rambling discourse on delivery protocols, as if tomorrow I'm assuming office as the new minister for courier mail.

The satchel bears an assortment of flat and fat plastic-sealed packages; this neighborhood, and that, and the other. Many insane names that must've scarred their owners since childhood.

Hooky thankfully ceases his one-man symposium. "Okay then," he says, getting to his feet. "Keep the moped at your place and I'll drop by tomorrow."

Ticktick, ticktick. Is it a watch? No, a beating heart. Systole, diastole, systole, diastole: it's coming from among the packages.

"All well?" Hooky asks with a bemused smile.

Is he deaf? My breath shortens into frantic puffs. A lumpy package, the shade of charcoal, addressed to one L. Luck. No effing way.

The parcel places flat against my ear. Yes, the ticking, it's emitting from inside the wrap. I flip it over and shake it a few times, but nothing of it strikes me as otherworldly.

Hooky leans toward me. "What's wrong?"

My hand outstretches the package to him. "Y-you ever deliver here?"

His brows squish together. "I've delivered to these apartments before, but never to this address. Does this block even exist?"

"No worries," I say, snatching the parcel from his paws. "I'll find my way."

My palms are sweaty when I'm repacking the satchel. The heavens have responded, Holliday. You're nearing the finish line, wherever that is, so long as it's not a bottomless pit.

The swollen late-day sun hangs low in the cloudless pink sky as I swerve into the guardhouse lane of my destination. I pull up Hooky's moped at its white barrier arm, my thin-soled loafers scraping against the blacktop lest I crash into metal. Then, wincing, I press my fingers against the scruff of my neck to soothe the smarting crick.

Goddammit, why is it every time I ride any mechanical contraption but my bicycle, I'm magnetically drawn toward cops on sidewalks? What'll happen if I get behind the wheel of a car? Will I mow over a company of marching army cadets? Whew, good thing I didn't decapitate the man. Who can afford attorneys these days? Either way, Holliday, inhale, exhale. You made it.

Beyond the barrier, a gather of stately beige towers with terracotta roofs festoon the sprawling apartment complex. The guardhouse leftward of me, though, looks deserted, which I find strange given the oppressive swank of the place. Hell, if I were the manager, I'd detail commandos wielding Kalashnikovs to guard the entrance.

"Hello? Package delivery," I say, craning my neck toward its window.

A pair of spooked eyes creep over the windowsill and our gazes meet. Soon after, a bald man shoots upright and slaps on his black beret.

Then his palms cover his eyes, and he's massaging their sockets in unhurried strokes, again and again thanking someone under his breath. "Yes?" he asks in a strained voice.

I adjust my boxcar helmet to raise its peaked visor above my brow. "Courier service, for the love of God. What're you doing, anyway?"

"Me? Oh, playing dead."

A suitably gruesome retort instantly springs to mind, but I stifle the urge. Focus, Holliday, you have no time for games.

"Where's Block E?"

Baldy peers at the horizon, scratching his upper lip. "There's a Block E?"

My chin droops toward the footrest, and I blow out my cheeks to make a popping sound. Useless, the lot of them. "Just raise the arm."

He's licking his lips and fidgeting with his belt as if it's biting into his belly. "Boss, for your sake, leave the package with me."

How does he know it's just one? A mirthless chortle expels from my throat. "Not a chance in hell. Why, though?"

Baldy glances sidelong at the towers, his flattish face turning ashen. "T-tambun J-jun."

"Eh? Is he a local outlaw? Why is he named after the neighborhood?"

"Much worse, my friend, much worse," Baldy says, gravely shaking his head. "He's the devil himself, only appears a child."

Humph, the security here is a much bigger letdown than expected. I bet a cardboard cutout of a weasel is immensely more reliable than scaredy-cat here. "For shame, a grown man wielding a billy club petrified of a brat."

He makes a pained face and points inside the complex. "You see that black stump? Used to be our mailbox. But his gang burned the mail so many times the post office struck it off their collection list."

"So what? I'm hand delivering."

Baldy wearily shrugs, then he stoops rightward and I hear the click of a button. "Try to return in one piece," he says as the barrier hikes upward.

I turn the ignition key, sneering at him. Guards scared of little brats, sheesh. What's next? Dogs terrified of mice?

The moped cruises downslope on a winding driveway that connects to a network of pristine marked lanes crisscrossing through the complex. Tin-roofed parking spaces abound beside the building blocks, bounded by lush medians painted black-and-yellow, and parading a multitude of flashy cars.

There's plenty to marvel over the moneyed life, and yet a strange ferment builds in my chest. Why is this place a ghost town? It only needs rolling tumbleweed and a wary old cowboy with his pistol drawn to complete the desolate look.

The tautness in my gut now slides to my bladder. Someone's watching me.

A slit-eyed boy with a fruit-bowl haircut. He's lazing on the shaded steps of the building I'm gliding by, his unyielding stare sending chills up my spine.

I rubberneck at him, scowling. You're not the boss of me, you little twerp. Was Baldy fretting over him? Bah, there's nothing a hearty whipping won't solve. Now, where's that damn Block E?

And then my bladder is twingeing, and I squirm on the sparsely padded saddle. Ack, this always happens when I'm stressed. I drift to the lane's shoulder and swing off the moped.

Plenty of dense shadowy thickets in the vicinity, and my business won't take but a minute. No sense suffering Baldy again for directions to the urinal.

Once more I tug on the cubic carrier's small padlock. Oh, stop it, Holliday. Baldy is a wimp, and so the kid bullies him. No way he'd dare mess with you.

But not long after, when I leap out from the bushes, the carrier's lid hangs open by its hinges. I race back and gape at the empty inside, at once torn between roaring and bawling, and so what escapes my lips is a sorry bleat. Goddammit, the thief took Lady Luck's package.

Dizzy, I pitch against the saddle for support, my loose jaw gulping air, a viselike numbness overpowering me. This is cruel, so effing cruel. Curses, cosmic joker, why can't you befool someone else for a change?

There's a pricking sensation on my forearm from the sticky note clinging to the saddle. I peel it off posthaste and upraise it to my nose. In stringy longhand, the note reads: *you've been Jun'd.*

Anger wells in me as magma in a pregnant volcano. Jun. Is that the demonic child? I crumple the note and chuck it to the asphalt before stamping on it over and over to channel my fury. What do I do now?

The crisp chime of bicycle bells tickles my ears before three sleek mountain bikes whizz past me upstreet. The kid with the fruit-bowl hair, Jun, I presume, slams his brakes a few yards away to wave the package in my direction, cockily grinning.

"You're dead, kid," I yell, bounding atop the moped and gunning its engine.

Jun's gang cackles before pedaling away with me in feverish pursuit. I'm darting left and right through the sinuous lanes in sight of their backs, the hems of their colorful tees fluttering in the wind, yet by and by it hits me something's very wrong.

Curses, how are these clowns zigging and zagging with such military precision? Screw this, I'll ram into the rascals if I must. I hunch forward in the seat and twist the throttle to its full rotation, to which the engine screeches in protest, lifting the front wheel for a hair-raising shake before I surge ahead.

They sense me closing in and their sass falters; now they're casting anxious looks over their shoulders, their pedaling so furious it blurs their feet.

My face finds a wicked smile. Soon enough I'll yank them off their bicycles, and with my helmet flog them to within an inch of their lives. Eh, what's this fool doing?

Jun is breaking away from his pals and swerving rightward to a tall seaweed-green trash can. In a flash his arm sticks out to pull on its thick rim, which promptly sends the receptacle tumbling onto the road, leaking out squat garbage bags and rolling dead in my path.

An anguished moan tears through my heart, yet it won't pry past my parched throat. I'm pumping the handbrakes nonstop, but they limply hiss, offering no resistance under my grip. Goddammit.

Fast-forward an atomic second and I'm too slow to cut off course, and so the moped's undercarriage clips the can and I lose control. Now we're ricocheting toward the median straddling the lanes, that is until the handbrakes awaken to their purpose, naturally at the most catastrophic moment.

The rust bucket's rear wheel levitates on a dime and launches me off the saddle. Time slows to a popsicle freezing when I'm flying bug-eyed into the no-parking sign beyond the median's concrete belt.

CLANG.

My spine bangs against its metal post, and I flump onto the trimmed grass, groaning and clutching my sides.

Their horselaughs are molten lead in my ears as I sob from pain. Why, why must I forever be doggy-paddling in an ocean of dung?

Sometime later, when blood returns to my limbs, I stagger to my feet and unstrap the helmet. The moped presents a sorry picture under the dusking sky; sprawled over the asphalt, deep slashes across its belly and its fender battered.

I mumble swears when lugging it upright. More money owed that I don't have. Bah, this up and I'll need a crash course in robbing banks.

A burst of red light blinds me and I flinch, shading my eyes. One of Jun's thugs is standing round twenty feet away, standing at the mouth of an alley cutting through the buildings, twisting a finger in his ear and pointing a laser pen at me. And underarm the mook clings to a parcel, my precious charcoal parcel.

Un-effing-believable. How low have I fallen for these sniveling do-rags of snot to taunt me fearlessly? My posture stiffens and the bottom of my bowels produce a bestial bare-teethed growl.

Now they've done it, burned through the microscopic affection for children which yet clung to my heart. My helmet clatters against the pavement and I march toward him, my limbs lashing front and back, waves of violent heat flushing through my body.

The kid scrams into the alleyway as I near, and headlong I follow him, breathing fire. "Stop and I'll spare your life," I holler at his silhouette, but he doesn't abide. Bah, I'm wasting my breath on these kids, they won't learn their lesson until I tan their backsides.

The alley is murkier than I expect, and so my brisk clip slackens to a crawl. Its spooky umbra fires up my imagination with a cast of hideous monsters, while the crunch of dry leaves underfoot makes my butterflies jitterbug. Courage, Holliday, a darkness that pales against your life is nothing to fear.

The boy is nearby with his back to me, whistling aimlessly while heeling against a droning air con unit and toying with my parcel. My dread swaps for fury as I tiptoe up to him, my fingers shaped into talons, and then I spring at his shoulder.

"Show's over, punk," I say, seizing my property, my claw digging into his shoulder blade. "Call the rest of your monkey crew to kiss my toes, and I promise no one gets hurt."

Any normal child should cower, but this one leers at me before swinging his instep to my shin. Ow! He flees while I'm hopping round on one leg, anguished cusses streaming out my lips. Welcome, Holliday, to your new low.

Behind me, the pitter-patter of footsteps approaches. "But someone will hurt today. Guess who?" says a small, husky voice oozing malice.

I wheel round in slo-mo, a colony of goose pimples sprouting on my arms. Jun and his cronies wear murderous looks, cracking their necks left and right, and flexing their fists fitted with brass knuckles.

My feet drag backward on their own, and I clutch Lady Luck's parcel tighter to my chest. Then I hold my palm out in their direction, sounding a nervous giggle. "Did I say kiss my toes? No, no, I meant I'll buy you Coke."

They keep their stark demeanors, now beating their loose fists into their palms, matching my pace as I retreat deeper into the alley.

My nethers are pinching, warning me they'll pummel me into mashed potatoes, then leave me bleeding by the burned mailbox.

Many times, I glimpse behind to the forbidding darkness, to its very distant pinprick of light, swallowing without pause. No point quitting now, Holliday, you're in the homestretch. Just remember, the abyss is your old friend.

Pant, pant. Blasted kids, don't they ever tire? Pant, pant. If I'm ever elected prime minister, my first order will be to allot them a firearm each and ship them off to war. If that doesn't rein their mischief, nothing will.

It's nightfall, the cicadas and crickets are chirping their mating calls, and I'm trudging up the last dozen steps to Block E's top floor. Ack, why did I miss this building my first five dashes round the complex?

The oblong lobby's checkerboard tiles are slicker than ice cubes, and thus skidding and sliding over them, I fall into the sing-song doorbell of Lady Luck's presumed apartment. Then I nip back to the stairwell to peek downstairs for signs of Satan's schoolkids. Whew. Safe, for now.

I drop to one knee to massage my tumid ankles, then drag my thumb over the three shades of muck coating my cheeks. Wish I'd taken the elevator, but then I risked the little gremlin Jun cutting power to the building. I've learned the hard way he possesses a talent for villainy unmatched in Malaysia.

Garbled voices, from a blaring TV I presume, strain outside from behind the tawny paneled door, but there's no hint of movement. Jeez, what's taking her so long? Should I ring the doorbell again?

No sooner does the thought cross my mind that the bolt unlatches, and in the doorway shows a middle-aged aunty with short wavy hair.

My pulse quickens upon sighting the huge mole on her chin. Lady Luck? Must be. I've never seen another soul with a facial blot the size of a dime.

Beaming, I skip toward her to present the parcel. "Special delivery."

Lady Luck silently accepts the package, and straightaway presses it against her ear. Shortly, she lowers it to her side and thrusts her open palm toward me.

I blink on repeat. She wants something? Oh! I flash out my wallet to retrieve the special dollar bill, and upon smoothing its creases, offer it with a wide grin.

But she ignores my gesture and continues outstretching her hand; her stare vacant, her eyes unblinking.

My fingers clench my thinning hair in clumps. "What? You want my kidneys or something?"

The neighboring door cracks open, creaking, to let a figure peek through the aperture. My eyes pronto bulge from shock. A capped dome and a wild corkscrewed beard. Impossible.

Yaya cranes his neck out the doorway bearing a rubbery smile, while behind him in the blackness sound the soft clopping of hoofs and the swishing of a long tail. "The clues, son. She wants proof of your quest," his talking head says.

My impulse to scold him for his absence abruptly fades, and instead my face forms a pout. Uh-oh, they're locked in the iron trunk under my bed. How ought I know she'd ask for them?

Yaya catches my expression and groans. "Can't you do anything right?" Then he looks to her and babbles a rapid-fire string of numbers.

I look askance at Yaya, convinced he's gone insane, but to my astonishment Lady Luck nods in agreement. She again holds out the parcel and next a shrill whistle carries from her lips.

My climbing blood pressure presents as a dull headache. Why, why is every unearthly creature I meet a complete crackpot? First Yaya and now Lady Luck. Curses.

Feet are pounding up the stairs, their slam-bang echo resounding in the lobby, and in sync my breath hitches and my limbs jam in place. The monster, he's here. I'm a goner.

Jun utters a feral cry and brushes past me, swiping the package from Lady Luck and racing into the apartment. Soon enough, I hear him tearing its wrap, followed by a lengthy bout of scrunching and stomping. Whatever lay inside is now mincemeat.

Lady Luck keeps her blank face through the commotion, then turns round and slams the door behind her. Yaya's been quiet for too long, and though his mysterious grin holds, I sense he's frozen as though someone hit pause on his cassette tape.

The monsters and messiahs are comrades, eh? Well played, God. Best celestial joke yet at my expense. Was my quest for naught, then? An errant knight's foolish fantasy? I slip to my haunches and palm my face, an infinite emptiness filling my soul.

Yaya is snickering. "You love making things difficult for yourself, huh?"

I cast him a beaten gaze. "What's going on here? Why doesn't she speak?"

He purposely looks away. "Um, let's just say it's spring-cleaning for both of us."

There's a click when the doorknob twists and then Lady Luck strides out the door, a folding clipboard tucked underarm, which she right away extends toward me.

Thereon, below the stringed pen, affixes a solitary sheet of orange paper with nothing but a six-digit number in a large font. Lady Luck meets my perplexed stare, flourishing her wrist as though she's painting spaghetti on an airy canvas.

"She wants you to sign at the bottom," Yaya says, gently neighing. "Why? To sign over my soul?" I ask, my lips pursing.

He clucks disapprovingly. "No, you idiot, to add you to her paper route. And for heaven's sake, remember that number."

The canvas bag from that day. "Lady Luck has a paper route…"

Yaya grunts his assent. "Yes, for the blessed. You think she has her gig without hard work? The big guy upstairs is very demanding."

I sign the form with hand atremble, then recoil when Lady Luck lunges for the clipboard the moment I'm done, and again tucking it underarm, she reverts to her motionless state.

"What about my lottery?" I ask, pulling erect and shifting from foot to foot.

Lady Luck throws up eight fingers, mumbling under her breath, to which Yaya grimly bobs his head.

My hands tie at my waist and I'm wringing them black-and-blue. Please, please don't say eight years.

"Eighth day of the week," she blurts.

"There are only—"

"Hang tight, son," Yaya interrupts. "Soon we'll lose enough people to add a day or two."

What the hell does that even mean? "W-what must I do?"

He shrugs nonchalantly. "Be grateful you'll live? Also, and this is crucial, tell Baldy your number before heading home so he won't reap your soul tonight."

Huh? My ears are ringing when I swallow the barf licking the tail of my throat. I…they've…

Yaya harrumphs, his eyes twinkling. "Allow me."

And presto, there's a knock-knock in my head. The annoying little man is laughing in the geezer's voice, and then he declares: Damn you, Holliday. Now you're forty and still a fool.

⌘

Acknowledgment

I am eternally beholden to my beloved wife, Jerrica, for her unflagging love and patience in helping me complete the manuscript. Doubtless, I'd never have crossed the finish line without her keen editorial commentary and unwavering faith in these stories. She also cocreated the book's protagonists *Kalia* and *Holliday*.